The Bobbsey Twins' Wonderful Secret

BY
LAURA LEE HOPE
AUTHOR OF "THE BOBBSEY TWINS SERIES,"

NEW YORK
GROSSET & DUNLAP
PUBLISHERS

Made in the United States of America

CONTENTS

CHAPTER		PAGE
I	THE SATIN PILLOW	1
II	SOMETHING QUEER	13
III	THE BOY IN THE CELLAR . . .	25
IV	ANOTHER SECRET	36
V	ON THE TRAIL	46
VI	NAN'S ORANGE TIE	54
VII	FREDDIE'S MISTAKE	66
VIII	STRANGE VOICES	75
IX	LOCKED IN	86
X	WINTER FUN	99
XI	THROUGH THE ICE	111
XII	THE SNOWBALL FIGHT	120
XIII	CHRISTMAS SHOPPING	128
XIV	FLOSSIE'S CAKE	136
XV	FREDDIE'S TUMBLE	147
XVI	NAN'S DISAPPOINTMENT . . .	154
XVII	BERT'S QUEER TALK	162
XVIII	DISCOVERED	172
XIX	CAUGHT IN THE SNOW	179
XX	THE BEAR SONG	188
XXI	AUNT SALLIE PRY	197
XXII	NEW PLANS	208
XXIII	WHERE ARE THE TWINS? . . .	215
XXIV	SAFE FROM THE STORM	227
XXV	MERRY CHRISTMAS SECRETS . .	234

THE BOBBSEY TWINS' WONDERFUL SECRET

CHAPTER I

THE SATIN PILLOW

Bang! Clatter! Bang!

That was Freddie Bobbsey hurrying down the cellar stairs as fast as he could go.

Clippity! Clatter! Clop!

Flossie Bobbsey, the twin sister of Freddie, made almost as much noise as did the small boy, with his yellow, curling hair and blue eyes that seemed to be dancing with a queer light this morning.

"Ha! Ha! Ha!" laughed Freddie Bobbsey.

"Ho! Ho! Ho!" laughed Flossie Bobbsey.

The small twins were down in the cellar now, moving about among the boxes, barrels, and other things that are kept under the

1

house. The voices of Freddie and Flossie floated up to the kitchen where jolly, fat, black Dinah Johnson, the cook, was busy.

"Dem honey lamb chilluns suah am havin' one gran' time wif de secret!" chuckled Dinah as she stirred the batter for a cake and between the beatings of the spoon listened to the voices of the twins in the cellar. "Yes, indeedy! Dey suah is havin' a gran' time wif de secret!"

"Whut secret am dat, Dinah?" asked Sam, her husband. He had come in the house to get a drink of water, having been working out in the garage over the Bobbsey automobile. "Whut yo' mean—secret?"

"Ho! Am dat yo', Sam?" asked Dinah, just as if she didn't know her own husband. She kept on beating up the cake batter.

"Suah it's me!" answered Sam. "Whut yo' all think?"

"Oh, I don' know," chuckled Dinah. "Whut yo' all want?"

"A drink ob water, fo' one thing," answered Sam. "But whut's dis I done heah yo' say 'bout a secret Flossie an' Freddie got down in de cellar?"

"Secret?" murmured Dinah, pretending not to understand.

"Suah, secret!" retorted her husband. "I done heah yo'!"

"Oh, secret!" Dinah was laughing now. She set the bowl of cake batter on the kitchen table, went to the oven to see if it was hot enough, and came back to say: "Yo' know whut a secret is, don't yo', Sam Johnson?"

"Suah I knows whut a secret is. It's suffin dat yo' ain't s'posed to tell."

"Dat's right!" chuckled Dinah. "An' I ain't a-goin' to tell dis secret of Flossie an' Freddie. So now yo' got yo' drink ob water, Sam, yo' kin shuffle back to de autymobile," and Dinah began pouring the cake batter into pans to put in the oven.

"Hu!" muttered Sam as he went out. "I'll find out dat secret by mahse'f, anyhow. Dat's whut I will!"

Up the cellar stairs came running Flossie and Freddie. They were full of jolly laughs and giggles. Dinah turned to look at them as she closed the oven door.

"Whut now?" asked the old colored cook, who had also been a sort of nurse when Fred-

die and Flossie were little and had served
in the same way when the older twins, Bert
and Nan, were smaller than Flossie and Freddie were now. "Yo' all want suffin'?" asked
Dinah.

"Please could we have a little milk?" asked
Flossie.

"Suah!" Dinah answered.

"And some meat," added Freddie.

"No meat—it's too soon!" Dinah said.
"Milk am all right but no meat."

"All right," Freddie agreed.

Then, with Flossie carrying the milk and
both of them giggling, the small twins again
started down cellar.

"Don't you push me and make me spill
this!" warned Flossie.

"No, I won't!" Freddie promised.

For once the small twins were in accord.
They were not disputing, as they often did
when Freddie wanted to squirt water from his
toy fire engine and Flossie wouldn't get out
of his way with her family of dolls. Whatever
the secret was that Flossie and Freddie had
down cellar, they were working together over
it, in "sweet peace an' joy," as Dinah said.

Sam Johnson, who had come to a stop outside the kitchen door after getting his drink of water, heard this talk between his wife and the smaller Bobbsey twins. The colored chauffeur shook his head in puzzlement as he murmured:

"Dey's suffin' queer goin' on 'round dish yeah place! Whut fo' Flossie an' Freddie takin' milk down cellar? Whut fo' Freddie ast fo' meat an' Dinah say it's too soon fo' meat? Dat's queer! I's gwine to take a look down in dat cellar."

Sam was close to the outside cellar door, down which Flossie and Freddie often slid when they had on their old clothes. The colored man, glancing toward the kitchen to make sure his wife was not looking at him from a window, went softly toward the door and tried to raise it. But he could not.

"Locked!" he murmured. "It suah mus' be a big secret to make dem twins lock de do'! But I'll find out!"

Talking to himself, Sam went back to the garage. Meanwhile Flossie and Freddie were very busy down cellar. Flossie had managed to get down safely without being "jiggled" by her brother so none of the milk was spilled. After a while the little twins came clattering up the stairs again and into Dinah's kitchen.

"Whut now?" asked the colored cook, smiling.

"Could we have this piece of old blanket?" asked Flossie.

"Suah!" was the answer.

"It's nice and soft," said Freddie as he took hold of one corner. "I'll carry it down, Flossie."

"No! I'm going to take it!" insisted the little girl.

"It's my turn!" said Freddie, firmly. "You carried the milk so I'm going to carry this blanket. Dinah, make Flossie give it to me."

"Oh, all right!" suddenly agreed Flossie. "Take it!"

She let go her hold on the soft piece of cloth and Freddie hurried down cellar with it, followed by his sister. Flossie whispered something in her brother's ear.

"Bert and Nan are out in the back yard," said Flossie. "We don't want them to know the secret."

"Sure not!" agreed Freddie.

Perhaps the sight of Bert and Nan had caused Flossie to end so suddenly the dispute about the blanket. It would never do to let the older twins find out so soon! A secret isn't any fun unless it is kept a long time.

Through the open window, Bert and Nan had seen the small twins hurrying about and darting down cellar with something.

"What do you suppose they are doing now?" asked Nan as Bert got out the croquet set, for he and his sister had decided to have a game.

"Don't know," Bert answered, without showing much interest.

"They've been chasing up and down cellar half a dozen times this morning," went on Nan.

"They're always doing something," said Bert.

"But this is different," proceeded Nan. "I saw Flossie taking a cup of milk down."

"Oh, then they're playing one of their games," decided Bert. "They may be playing house, or store, or shipwrecked on a desert island."

"I suppose so," Nan agreed. "But maybe I'd better take a look."

"What for?"

"To make sure everything is all right. They may get into trouble."

"Oh, Dinah is right there," said Bert. "Come on and have a game. I'll give you first shot."

"Well, all right," murmured Nan, doubtfully. She looked toward the closed cellar door, wondered what Flossie and Freddie could be doing down the dark place, and then took her croquet mallet.

All this time Flossie and Freddie were very busy down in the cellar. As she watched the baking of her cake, Dinah could hear the murmur of their voices coming up to her through the floor.

"Honey lambs!" murmured the old colored woman. "Bress dey hearts! I jes lubs 'em!"

As Dinah was taking the cake out of the oven and letting it fill the kitchen with a warm, spicy perfume, Flossie came hurrying up the steps again. This time Freddie did not follow. Flossie saw an old shawl on a chair in the corner. Sam sometimes used it in winter to put over the radiator of the automobile. He had brought it in the house to have Dinah wash it, for winter was coming on again now and it would be needed to keep the radiator from freezing when the car was left out.

"This old shawl isn't any good, is it, Dinah?" asked Flossie.

"Lan' sakes, honey, no!" Dinah exclaimed, being in a hurry to set the cake on the table, for the pan was hot.

"Then I'll take it," decided the little girl. "It's sort of cold down cellar, even if the furnace is going."

"Yes, 'tis gettin' cold," Dinah agreed. "I hope Bert an' Nan don't catch de sniffles out dere playin' croquet."

"Oh, are they playing croquet?" asked Flossie. "Freddie and I tried it the other day but the ground was so hard we couldn't put the wickets in."

"Dey's been a thaw since den," said Dinah. "But it's gittin' cold ag'in an' Bert an' Nan got to be keerful. Whut was it yo' done ast me, Flossie? I was thinkin' so much about mah cake an' Bert an' Nan playin' croquet in de cold dat I didn't give much heed."

"I asked if I could take this old shawl," said Flossie, who was already on her way down cellar with it.

"Oh, yes, I guess so," said Dinah. "Sam done brought it in but I clean forgot whut he tole me 'bout it. Go ahead, take it, Flossie."

So Flossie took it. Down into the cellar she hurried to a corner where Freddie was waiting for her.

"I guess this will be enough," Flossie said, holding up the shawl.

"Oh, sure! That's fine!" was her brother's answer. "Now we can fix up a dandy place."

Never had the small Bobbsey twins shared such a delightful secret before. Dinah was the only one who knew anything about it. Out in the yard where, though it was early December, the grass was still green, Bert and Nan knocked the croquet balls about. There had been a few flurries of snow the week before, but a warm spell had followed and it was still possible for Mr. Bobbsey to play golf occasionally, while the four Bobbsey twins had not yet put away the croquet set.

"I'd like to know what Flossie and Freddie are up to," murmured Nan as she banged

Bert's ball, thereby gaining an extra shot for herself.

"Why bother about it?" he asked. "Let them play."

"Oh, if it's only play it's all right," Nan agreed. "But I think it is queer the way they keep taking things down cellar all the while."

"They have to have some place to play," remarked Bert as he whacked his ball to get back into position out of which Nan had knocked him. "They can't play in the garage on account of Sam's working on the car. So let them use the cellar."

"Yes, I suppose so," agreed Nan. "Especially as we want to use the garage ourselves. Don't you think we ought to make another try at it, Bert?"

"Yes, I guess so," answered her brother, looking around to make sure no one was listening. "But we can't do anything while Sam is in there. He'd be sure to hear us and tell."

"Oh, yes! We have to wait until he gets out of the way," agreed Nan. "And so, maybe, it's just as well Flossie and Freddie have their secret down cellar."

"So that we can have ours out in the garage!" chuckled Bert. "That's right, Nan! Go on! It's your shot and you're dead on me."

"Yes, so I am! Well, we've got to do something soon. And if Sam doesn't get out of the garage we'll have to go up in the attic."

"They'll hear us there."

"That's so. Well, we'll have to find some place."

The croquet game went on merrily. Flossie and Freddie continued their mysterious doings and whisperings down cellar, Dinah began putting chocolate on her cake, and Mrs. Bobbsey came hurrying out to the kitchen.

"Dinah!" exclaimed the mother of the twins, "have you seen my rose sofa pillow?"

"Your rose soffy piller, Mrs. Bobbsey?" questioned the cook.

"Yes. It was on the living room sofa a little while ago and now it is gone. The window was open, and it could easily have been reached from the porch. Dear me! I hope no tramp came along and took my lovely pillow!"

"Are you suah it's gone?" asked Dinah.

'Yes, it's gone!" said Mrs. Bobbsey. "I wonder what could have happened to it?"

CHAPTER II

SOMETHING QUEER

Dinah kept on spreading rich, brown chocolate on top of the cake she had just baked. Mrs. Bobbsey looked at her cook and seemed to think there was something queer about Dinah. So she asked:

"You haven't taken my lovely, rose pillow, have you?"

"Oh, no'm! Indeedy I hasn't!" said Dinah quickly.

"You didn't hear any tramp come up on the porch and take it, did you, Dinah?"

"Oh, no'm! Indeedy I didn't, Mrs. Bobbsey!"

"Well, I wonder where it could have gone? Perhaps Bert or Nan may have taken it. Where are they?"

"Bert an' Nan am playin' croquet in de yard," Dinah answered. "But I's feared maybe it's too cold for 'em."

"Oh, I hardly think so," Mrs. Bobbsey remarked. "They are moving about. But it seems rather strange to be playing croquet so near Christmas."

"It suah am queer weather we's havin' now," said Dinah as she spread another dab of chocolate on the cake.

"I'm not so much interested in the weather as I am in my lost sofa pillow," went on Mrs. Bobbsey. "I don't see what could have become of it. What's that noise?" she asked, suddenly.

"Dat's Flossie an' Freddie, I reckon," Dinah answered, slowly.

"Where are they, Dinah?"

"Down in de cellar."

"What are they doing there? I'll go see! They may be into some mischief," said Mrs. Bobbsey, quickly, as she stepped toward the door that led from the kitchen into the cellar.

"No'm, Mrs. Bobbsey! Don't go down there!" cried Dinah, dropping the chocolate-covered knife and stepping toward the twins' mother.

"Don't go down there? Why not?" asked

Mrs. Bobbsey in surprise. "Is anything the matter? Tell me quickly, Dinah! Has anything happened to my little twins? I must go down and see!"

"No'm! Yo' mustn't go down cellar!" said Dinah firmly, taking hold of Mrs. Bobbsey's arm. "Flossie an' Freddie dey is all right. But please stay up out ob dat cellar!"

"Dinah, there is something queer going on here and I must find out what it is!" exclaimed Mrs. Bobbsey. "I am going down cellar!"

But before she could start down the steps there came a loud cry from Nan who was playing croquet with Bert in the yard. It was followed by a crash of glass.

"Oh! Oh! Look what you did!" shouted Nan, and Mrs. Bobbsey, wishing to see what had happened, stepped away from the cellar door and hurried to the window. A look of relief came over Dinah's face.

Now that there is a pause for a moment, and while Mrs. Bobbsey is seeking to learn the reason for Nan's outcry, this opportunity will be taken to tell new readers something of the four children who are to have parts in this story.

There were four Bobbsey twins, as you have already seen. Bert and Nan were the older pair. They were tall, strong children, healthy and happy from much living out of doors. Their dark brown hair and brown eyes were quite different from the light hair and blue eyes of Flossie and Freddie, the younger twins.

Mr. and Mrs. Richard Bobbsey lived with their four twin children in the Eastern city of Lakeport on Lake Metoka, where Mr. Bobbsey owned a large lumber yard.

In the first book of this series, called "The Bobbsey Twins," you read how Flossie and Freddie and Bert and Nan had many good times around their home, where fat Dinah Johnson did the cooking and Sam, her husband, worked about the place. Snap, the dog, and Snoop, the cat, added to the fun the Bobbsey twins had, but now both dog and cat were getting old and were not as lively as they had been.

With their father and mother, and sometimes with their playmates, the Bobbsey twins

went on many journeys in the summer vaca-
tions. Grace Lavine and Nellie Parks were the
girls with whom Nan most often played, while
for his chums Bert had John Marsh, Charlie
Mason and Danny Rugg. Once upon a time
Danny and Bert had been enemies, but now
they were friends. Joe Norton and Sammie
Todd, however, though often friendly with
Bert and his chums, sometimes played tricks
on them.

As her special chums, Flossie had Susie
Larker and Mary Wenton, while for his particular boy friends Freddie had Harry Ford
and Ted Blake.

Going to the country, to the seashore, to
Snow Lodge, taking a trip on a house boat,
journeying to Cloverbank and Cherry Corners, and, once, taking part in a treasure
hunt, kept the four Bobbsey children busy
having good times.

The book just before this one you are now
reading is called "The Bobbsey Twins at
Spruce Lake," and the story tells how Mr.
Bobbsey went to a place up in the woods to
buy a lumber tract from a man named Jake
Doxey. There was something strange about

Mr. Doxey for he could not be found. In searching for him Mr. Bobbsey was nearly shipwrecked in a motor boat when caught in a storm. Many things also happened to the Bobbsey twins and they had a strange adventure with a runaway boy.

The Bobbsey family remained in camp at Spruce Lake all summer before Jake Doxey could be found and the lumber tract bought. Then the children and their parents returned to Lakeport, for it was time for the twins to go back to school. The Christmas holidays were now approaching and with them came two secrets, one being shared by Bert and Nan and the other by Flossie and Freddie. Neither pair of twins knew what the other's secret was.

But now something else besides secrets seemed to be in the air, for Mrs. Bobbsey had missed her lovely rose satin sofa pillow. Dinah, for some reason, did not want the mother of Flossie and Freddie to go down the cellar to see what the small twins were doing, and Nan had screamed out in the yard, following the sound of crashing glass.

"What is it, Nan? What happened?" asked

Mrs. Bobbsey, quickly opening the kitchen window and looking at the two children who had been playing croquet in the yard. "Is anyone hurt?"

"No, Mother," Bert answered, swinging his mallet. "It's all right."

"But he gave his ball an awful whack when he didn't make the last wicket," reported Nan, "and he broke a pane of glass in the garage."

"No I didn't!" said Bert.

"Yes you did!" cried Nan. "I heard it smash!"

"It was only an old piece of glass standing up against the garage," Bert said. "It was a piece left over after Sam mended the window I broke playing ball."

"Oh!" said Nan.

"Oh! Got left, didn't you, Smarty!" mocked Bert.

"Children!" called Mrs. Bobbsey, "please be polite."

"Well, I don't care. I heard the glass smash," went on Nan.

"And you yelled like a Wild West Indian!" chuckled Bert. "I didn't do any harm."

"Maybe not," his mother said, from the window. "But I heard you hit your croquet ball very hard, Bert, and it might have hurt some one. You must be careful."

"He was mad because he didn't go through the last wicket!" Nan taunted.

"I was not! I don't care!" exclaimed Bert. "Croquet isn't any fun, anyhow! I'm going to get John Marsh and Charlie Mason and kick my football."

"You're mad because I beat you! Mad because I beat you!" mocked Nan, dancing around the yard swinging her mallet.

"I am not!" retorted Bert.

"Children, please stop!" ordered Mrs. Bobbsey, and when she spoke in that tone Bert and Nan knew it was best to obey. "And please come to the window," went on their mother. "I want to ask you something."

"Oh, I hope it isn't about what we have been doing in the garage!" Nan quickly whispered to her brother.

"No. I don't believe she knows a thing about that," Bert said in a low voice.

"Have either of you seen my new rose sofa

pillow?" asked Mrs. Bobbsey when Nan and Bert stood beneath the window.

"Your sofa pillow?" Nan repeated, wonderingly.

"Yes. It is missing from the couch in the living room, and I saw it there this morning when I opened the window to air the place. Did you take it?"

"Why, no, Mother!" murmured Nan, looking at her brother in surprise and wonderment.

"What would I do with a rose-colored sofa pillow?" asked Bert.

"I can't imagine," his mother said with a smile. "But I felt I had better ask you. And I must ask Flossie and Freddie. I hope no tramp slipped up on the porch and took the pillow out of the open window."

"Oh, Mother! That would be terrible!" exclaimed Nan.

"I'd like to catch a tramp doing that!" blustered Bert. "I'd fix him!"

"Flossie and Freddie are down cellar, Mother," went on Nan as Bert hurried around to the front of the house for a possible sight of a pillow-taking tramp.

"Yes, I know they are," said Mrs. Bobbsey. "And that is also something queer. When I wanted to go down cellar to ask Flossie and Freddie if they had seen my pillow, Dinah didn't want me to."

"She didn't?" exclaimed Nan. "Why?"

"I don't know. But she seemed much excited."

"Oh, I guess they're just playing store or some of their games down there," Nan said with a smile. "I saw Flossie carrying down a cup of milk."

"Then I suppose it is all right," Mrs. Bobbsey said. "But I can't understand why Dinah should act so queerly about it. However, I am going down to see what my little twins are doing, and I want to ask them about my lovely, lost pillow."

Mrs. Bobbsey was spared the trouble of going down cellar after Flossie and Freddie, for when she turned back again into the kitchen, after closing the window, the small twins were already in the room.

"What made Nan yell?" asked Flossie.

"We heard her when we were down cellar," added Freddie.

"Oh, Bert hit his croquet ball rather hard and it broke an old piece of glass leaning against the garage," explained Mrs. Bobbsey.

"I thought maybe it was a fire," went on Freddie. "So I came up to get my engine and squirt on it to put it out."

"No, there isn't any fire, thank goodness," said Mrs. Bobbsey. "But what are you two doing down cellar?" she asked with a smile. "It seems very queer and mysterious. Dinah didn't want me to go down." She looked for the colored cook, but Dinah had left the kitchen. If Mrs. Bobbsey had been looking she might have seen Dinah hurrying down the cellar steps as Flossie and Freddie came up.

Then Mrs. Bobbsey remembered about her lost pillow and asked:

"You twins didn't take it, did you?"

"What?" asked Flossie and Freddie together.

"My rose sofa pillow—that new one," their mother replied. "It is missing from the couch in the living room. If you have it——"

Just then the telephone rang and Mrs. Bobbsey hurried away to answer it. She did not see the strange look that passed between the small twins when she had spoken of the rose sofa pillow.

"Oh! Oh!" murmured Freddie as his mother hurried into the hall where the telephone bell was jingling.

"If ever she finds out!" murmured Flossie. "Come on, Freddie, let's go outside!" she whispered.

CHAPTER III

THE BOY IN THE CELLAR

MRS. BOBBSEY found that the telephone call was from one of her lady friends who wanted her to go shopping that afternoon.

"It is getting close to Christmas," said Mrs. Parks over the telephone when Mrs. Bobbsey hurried to answer it.

"Indeed it is," agreed the mother of the twins. "I shall be glad to go down town with you and look through the stores. I may have to buy a new sofa pillow."

"What became of that lovely rose one?" asked Mrs. Parks.

"It seems to have disappeared most mysteriously," replied Mrs. Bobbsey. "I was just asking my children about it when you 'phoned. I hope no tramp stole it."

"Oh, goodness! I hope not!" exclaimed Mrs. Parks. "All right, then, I'll stop for you in my car this afternoon."

Mrs. Bobbsey turned away from the telephone and, looking from a side window, saw Flossie and Freddie running across the yard. At the same time she saw Sam come out of the garage, and then Bert and Nan made a dash for the building where the automobile was kept. Flossie and Freddie followed the older twins.

"Go on back!" ordered Bert.

"No!" retorted Freddie.

"Yes, you must! Bert and I have something special to do in the garage," said Nan.

"Oh, is it a secret?" asked Flossie, her eyes shining.

"Never mind what it is," chuckled Bert. "You two can go on playing down cellar as you were."

"We've finished down there," Freddie answered. "Haven't we?" and he turned to his blue-eyed sister.

"Yes," said Flossie. "For a while, anyhow."

"Well, you can't come in the garage!" declared Bert.

"We have just as good a right in there as you have," insisted Freddie. "So we're going in! Come on, Flossie!"

"No, you two mustn't come in," said Nan, firmly, but gently. "After a while we'll let you in."

"We're going in now!" cried Freddie. "Anyhow, I left my fire engine in there and I'm going to get it."

"I'll hand it out to you," offered Bert.

"I'll get it myself!" said Freddie who was very independent.

Mrs. Bobbsey, hearing the talk and fearing that the twins might get into a little quarrel, hurried out into the yard.

"There seems to be a great deal going on today," she said with a smile. "I don't know what it's all about, but, first of all, I must ask you about my lost sofa pillow."

"We didn't take it, did we, Nan?" asked Bert, quickly.

"Oh, no," Nan answered, edging toward the side door of the garage which Sam had left open when he went out.

"What about you, Flossie and Freddie?" asked their mother, turning to the smaller twins.

Mrs. Bobbsey, as well as Bert and Nan, was quite surprised at the strange way in which Flossie and Freddie looked at each other. They seemed to be worried and uneasy. But before they had a chance to say anything, Dinah called from the kitchen door:

"Mrs. Bobbsey!"

"Yes, Dinah, what is it? The telephone?"

"No'm! Dish ain't nuffin 'bout no telly-foam," answered the old cook. "But yo' rose soffy piller am done back on de couch."

"My sofa pillow back in place! Why, how did it happen? Where did it come from? Did the tramp bring it back?"

"No'm, Mrs. Bobbsey, it wasn't no tramp," said Dinah, wiping her hands on her apron as she stood in the kitchen door. "I put it back mah own se'f."

"You, Dinah! Did you have my nice cushion?"

Not waiting for an answer, Mrs. Bobbsey hurried into the house, followed by Nan and Bert and by the smaller twins. Flossie and Freddie kept looking at each other strangely, and Flossie murmured:

"Dinah must have brought it up."

"Yes," agreed Freddie. "But don't say anything—yet."

Into the front living room of the house hurried Mrs. Bobbsey. As she entered the door, followed by the twins and Dinah, she saw her much prized rose satin pillow in place on the couch.

"Oh, I'm so glad it is back!" Mrs. Bobbsey said. "But where did you find it, Dinah? Oh, see! It is soiled!" she exclaimed. "It has been in the dirt and someone tried to clean it —with gasoline!" she added.

The odor of gasoline was strong around the cushion which plainly showed where an effort had been made to freshen it up.

"Yes'm, I cleaned it," said Dinah. "It was kinda soiled."

"But who did it? Who had it?" exclaimed Mrs. Bobbsey. "If it was some tramp——"

Dinah looked at Flossie and Freddie. It was time for the small twins to speak.

"We had your cushion, Mother," confessed Flossie. "We took it to play with, but we didn't mean to get it dirty."

"And Dinah said we'd better bring it back," went on Freddie. "We didn't know you liked it so much, Mother."

"It is one of my best pillows," Mrs. Bobb-

sey said. "It is too bad it was soiled. But I
had rather lose it altogether than to have you
two little twins keep silent about it after you
took it. I am glad you told me the truth. But
you should not have taken it. What were you
doing with it?"

Flossie looked at Freddie and Freddie
looked at Flossie. Finally the little boy murmured:

"We—we were just sort of—playing with
it."

"Well," said his mother with a smile, "I
wish you hadn't taken it, but it is too late
for that now. Perhaps the dirt will come off.
You had better try some more gasoline,
Dinah."

"Yes'm. I will. I didn't hab much time to
clean it after I done found out dat Flossie an'
Freddie hab yo' piller. I done tole 'em to bring
it back, but dey runned out in de yard when
Bert cracked dat glass, so I got de piller
mahse'f an' tried to clean it."

"That was good of you, Dinah. Perhaps
with a little more gasoline it may clean up
nicely. Try it, please. And, after this, don't

take my good pillows or cushions to play with, Flossie and Freddie."

"No'm, we won't!" promised the younger twins.

Dinah took the sofa pillow out in the yard and Flossie and Freddie breathed easier. They felt quite bad over what had happened. Seeing that the two small twins were not going out again, Bert and Nan slipped away to the garage while Mrs. Bobbsey began to get ready to go down town with Mrs. Parks and see about the Christmas shopping.

"Let's go down cellar again," proposed Freddie to his sister after a while.

"All right," Flossie agreed.

As they passed through the kitchen they saw Dinah with the sofa pillow under her arm and a bottle of gasoline in one hand, going out into the yard.

"Whut I done tell yo', honey lambs?" questioned the old colored woman. "I done tole yo' not to play wif dis yeah cushion, didn't I?"

"Yes, Dinah, you did," said Flossie meekly.

"And we won't do it any more," promised Flossie.

"Anyhow, we don't need it now 'cause we have that piece of that big blanket and the old shawl," went on Freddie.

"Well, see dat yo' don't!" cautioned Dinah as she began to make another attempt to clean the rose pillow.

Flossie and Freddie went down cellar so they did not hear or see what Bert and Nan were doing out in the garage. And it was something strange enough, as the smaller twins found out later.

Bert and Nan were so busy over their own particular secret that they had no time to wonder what took Flossie and Freddie down cellar so often. And you may be sure the small twins were not going to tell.

"It'll be wonderful though, won't it?" whispered Freddie to his sister.

"Oh, so wonderful!" murmured the little girl. "And won't she be surprised? Mother, I mean!"

"Yes, and Daddy too!"

"Oh, I can hardly wait!" sighed Flossie.

"Neither can I," agreed her brother. "Let's take another look."

So they took another look. Now they did

not care what Nan and Bert were doing out in the garage.

That afternoon, it being Saturday, with no school, after coming up from the cellar, Flossie and Freddie went to play with some of their little friends at the home of Susie Larker. Bert and Nan, after having spent some time, most mysteriously, in the garage, went to a movie with John Marsh and Grace Lavine.

Mrs. Bobbsey came back from her Christmas shopping trip later that afternoon and found all four of her twins at home, for it was getting dark.

"Dinah cleaned the rose sofa pillow so you'd never know it had been dirty," Flossie reported.

"Did she, dear? I'm glad of that," answered her mother. "But you will not take it again, will you?"

"Oh, no'm!"

"We don't need it 'cause we have an old shawl and a blanket," said Freddie.

"What are you two doing with old shawls and blankets?" asked Nan, with a look at Bert.

"Oh, that's our secret!" said Flossie, with a laugh.

Just then Mr. Bobbsey came in from his lumber yard office and, as usual, there was a rush of the four twins to greet him, so all such things as secrets and sofa pillows were forgotten for a time.

"You look tired, my dear," said Mr. Bobbsey to his wife as Dinah announced the evening meal.

"I have been doing a little Christmas shopping," was the answer.

"My! My! Is Christmas so near as all that?" exclaimed Mr. Bobbsey. "How fast time goes! Why, it only seems a few weeks ago that we were at Spruce Lake."

"Didn't we have dandy times there?" cried Bert.

"Oh, I'll say we did!" echoed Nan.

"And wasn't it queer when we thought Daddy was lost?" asked Freddie.

"And it was queer when I was lost," added Bert.

"Yes, we had some exciting times at Spruce Lake," their father said. "But now we are settled down for the winter."

"Maybe we'll have some exciting times here," suggested Nan.

"I hope so," murmured Bert.

The evening was spent in talking about past adventures, and then, when Flossie and Freddie went up to their beds, Bert and Nan played a game. At last all the family had retired for the night.

What time it was Flossie did not know, but it was dark night when she heard a tap at her door.

"Who—who's there?" she whispered, sitting up in bed.

"Sh! Don't make a noise!" warned Freddie. "But I just looked down out of my window, Flossie, and I saw a boy crawling in the cellar window. We better go down there to see he doesn't take our secret."

"A boy—a boy getting into our cellar?" asked Flossie in a low voice.

"Yes," went on Freddie. "Come on! Let's go down and catch him!"

CHAPTER IV

ANOTHER SECRET

Flossie Bobbsey reached out to a chair beside her bed, got her bathrobe, and, feeling along under the edge of her bed with her bare feet, found her slippers. In a moment she was ready to join Freddie. He, also, had on bathrobe and slippers.

"How did it happen?" whispered Flossie as she went softly down the hall beside her brother towards Freddie's room. From his window one could look down to a small window that opened into the cellar. And in the dark basement, under this cellar window, was hidden the secret of the smaller Bobbsey twins. "How did it happen?" asked Flossie again, as her brother did not answer.

"What do you mean—happen?" he asked in a low voice for they were then passing the bedroom of their parents.

"I mean, how did you happen to see the

boy getting in our cellar window?" asked
Flossie. They were now past their parents'
room and could talk more freely.

"I got up to get a drink of water," Freddie explained, "and then I went to my window to look out, 'cause the moon was nice and
bright. Then I looked down at the cellar window and I saw this boy crawling along on
his hands and knees."

"Oh, isn't that just terrible!" gasped Flossie. "What boy was it, Freddie?"

"I couldn't tell. Right away I came to tell
you. We'll find out who he is, though."

"And we'll stop him from getting our secret," added Flossie. "Let's go in your room
and look down now and see if he's there yet."

Into Freddie's room the small twins tip-
toed. Freddie looked out first, thrusting his
head over the sill, for the window was open
at night so he would have plenty of fresh air
in his bedroom.

"Yes, he's down there now!" Freddie whispered, drawing in his head.

"Oh, let me look!"

Flossie pulled her brother aside and took
his place. Plainly, in the bright, silvery light

of the moon, she saw the dark figure of a boy groping around on his hands and knees near the cellar window, close to the precious secret.

"Oh!" murmured Flossie. And again: "Oh, Freddie!"

"Come on!" whispered the little boy. "We'll get him!"

"Is that cellar window locked?" Flossie wanted to know as they went softly into the hall again.

"I guess so," was Freddie's answer.

"Then that boy can't get in without breaking it," said Flossie. "And if he breaks it he'll make a noise and maybe a policeman will hear him and come and arrest him."

"Maybe," agreed Freddie. "But I'm going down and catch him now before he breaks the window."

"I'll go with you," bravely offered Flossie.

But something else happened just then. As the small twins were going down the back stairs to reach the kitchen, and so get into the cellar, a door opened and their father stepped into the hall. He seemed much surprised to see the two little twins and, as he turned up the hall light more brightly he asked:

"What are you two doing out here?"

For a moment neither Flossie nor Freddie knew what to say. But at last the little boy murmured:

"We're going to catch a boy."

"Catch a boy!" chuckled Mr. Bobbsey. "What's the matter with you two, anyhow? Are you dreaming and walking in your sleep?"

"We aren't asleep!" said Freddie.

"Of course we aren't!" added Flossie. "And we have to catch that boy before he—before he——" She hesitated. She did not want to speak of the secret in the cellar.

"What boy are you talking about?" asked Mrs. Bobbsey, appearing in the doorway back of her husband. "Dear me! You children must have been having queer dreams! Go back to your beds!"

"Oh, no, Mother! It was no dream!" said Flossie, quickly. "Freddie saw the boy first, and he waked me up and I saw him. He's trying to crawl in the side cellar window."

"Did you really see a boy?" asked Mr. Bobbsey, sure now that the twins were neither dreaming nor walking in their sleep.

"Oh, yes, I saw him!" declared Freddie.

"So did I!" added Flossie.

The door of Bert's room opened now and he came out in his bathrobe, rubbing his eyes sleepily.

"What's the matter?" he asked. "Is the place on fire?"

"Nonsense! Of course it isn't!" his mother said. "But the whole house will be roused in a moment. I suppose Nan will be the next to get up."

Hardly had she spoken when Nan, aroused by the talk in the hall, looked out of her bedroom.

"Oh, Bert!" she exclaimed as she saw her twin brother. "Is anything the matter out in the garage? Have they found out our sec——"

"Ahem!" coughed Bert, loudly, with a quick look at Nan and she did not finish what she was saying. But no one paid much attention to her for just then Freddie exclaimed:

"We'd better hurry up and catch that boy before he gets in our cellar window!"

"What boy?" asked Bert, quickly.

Then he was told what had happened. With quick steps he crossed the hall, looked out of Freddie's window and at once called:

"Golly! There is a boy down there. Hello, you!" he shouted. "Who are you and what are you doing?"

Mr. and Mrs. Bobbsey and the other children crowded into Freddie's room as Bert was calling down out of the window. Freddie was anxious to hurry on down cellar, as was Flossie, but Mrs. Bobbsey told them to wait a moment.

"Oh, hello, Bert!" answered the voice of the boy outside, down on the ground by the Bobbsey cellar window.

"Why, it's John Marsh!" Bert exclaimed.

"Sure! That's who I am!" said the boy.

"What's the matter, John?" went on Bert as he recognized one of his chums. The others waited for the answer.

"I lost my knife somewhere around your cellar window and I'm trying to find it," answered John. The Marsh family lived a few houses down the street.

"Lost your knife!" echoed Bert.

"Yes," went on John. "I was over at my aunt's house on the other side of town this evening," the boy explained. "I missed the last bus home so I had to walk. I was fooling with my knife as I passed here and it dropped out of my hand. I've been crawling around on the ground trying to find it, but I can't."

"I saw him crawling around," said Freddie. "I thought he was trying to get in our cellar window."

"My kid brother took you for a burglar, John!" said Bert with a laugh, as he leaned out of the window. "Wait a minute and I'll come down with my flashlight and help you look for your knife."

"Oh, don't bother," objected John. "I can look for it in the morning. I'm sorry if I scared your brother," he added.

"He didn't scare me any!" Freddie was quick to say, for he could hear what was said. "But I didn't want anybody to get in our cellar."

"Why not?" asked Bert, as he started for his room to get his flashlight.

"Oh—just—'cause," was all Freddie said as he gave Flossie a quick look.

"Well, I guess the excitement is over," said Mr. Bobbsey. "There isn't any burglar so you had better hop back into bed, Flossie and Freddie." Nan had already gone to her room when she found out what the disturbance was about. "And if you're going down to help John look for his knife, you'd better put on more clothes, Bert," he added.

"I will, yes, sir. But I won't be down there very long."

"It's getting colder," Mrs. Bobbsey warned him.

Bert slipped on his trousers and a coat and was soon outside the house, near the cellar window, shining the beam of his flashlight around on the ground.

"It's too bad to wake your folks up this way," said John as the two boys searched for the lost knife.

"Oh, that's all right," Bert answered. "What time is it, anyhow?"

"A little after twelve."

"Oh, I thought it was later—almost morning. There it is!" He suddenly pointed to something in a clump of grass close to the brick cellar wall.

"My knife! Oh, good!" cried John, picking it up. "Thanks a lot!"

"Now you're all right," remarked Bert.

"Sure! I didn't want to lose that knife. It's a good one. Well, I'll run along now. I hope your folks can get back to sleep," and John went down the street.

"Oh, we'll sleep all right," declared Bert. "So long!"

"So long!" echoed John.

"Be sure to lock that door when you come up," Bert's father called to him.

"Yes, sir, I did."

The Bobbsey house once more settled into the quiet of the night. Flossie got back into her bed, and Freddie into his. But before they went to their rooms the small twins said a few words to each other.

"I'm glad that boy didn't get in our cellar," remarked Flossie.

"So am I," agreed Freddie. "But, anyhow, John Marsh wouldn't take any of our secret."

"No, but we don't want even him to know about it."

"That's right, Flossie. And nobody knows about it yet except you and me and Dinah."

"Yes. Just us three!"

Flossie was settling down to sleep when she once more heard the shrill whisper of her twin brother at her door.

"Flossie!" called Freddie.

"Yes! what is it? Somebody else getting in the cellar?"

"No. But did you hear what Nan started to say about there being something in the garage?"

"Yes, I did," admitted Flossie. "I guess maybe there's another secret around here, Freddie."

"That's right. And I'm going to try to find out what it is. Nan and Bert have a secret too, I think!"

Before Flossie could reply Mrs. Bobbsey called:

"Go to sleep at once, you two! There's been enough excitement for one night."

So Flossie and Freddie went to sleep, wondering what might be the secret Bert and Nan had in the garage.

CHAPTER V

ON THE TRAIL

Nan Bobbsey came slowly out of the garage and walked toward the house. She knew her brother Bert was in the kitchen getting from Dinah a slice of bread and jam. It was Monday afternoon and on coming home from school Bert, who had hurried on ahead with Nan, had said he was hungry.

Flossie and Freddie had paused to speak to John Marsh, and Freddie, with a laugh, explained how he had, on Saturday night, seen the boy crawling around to find his lost knife and had mistaken him for a burglar.

"If you had been a burglar," said Freddie, "I might have squirted water on you from my fire engine."

"I'm glad you didn't," chuckled John.

It was because the smaller twins paused to talk to John that they did not get home with

Bert and Nan. And Bert had gone in the kitchen to get his bread and jam, while Nan hurried into the garage. Now Nan came out and, going to the kitchen door, she called:

"Come on, Bert! I'm waiting for you!"

"Be with you in a minute, Nan!" he answered. "Got that bread and jam ready yet, Dinah?"

"Heah it is!" murmured the fat, black cook. "Does yo' all want a piece too, Nan?" she asked.

"If you don't mind," Bert's sister answered.

"I'll bring it out," Bert offered.

"Be sure you don't take any bites off it!" warned Nan with a laugh.

"I'll be careful!" Bert promised. "Go on and get things ready and I'll be with you in a minute."

A little later, carrying two slices of bread and jam, at one of which he took big bites as he hurried along, Bert Bobbsey entered the garage where Nan already was waiting. Just then Flossie and Freddie came home from school.

"I wonder if we'd better take down any more things?" said Flossie to her twin brother.

"What things?" asked the little boy.

"Things for—for our secret," whispered Flossie. "I mean for our secret in the cellar."

"No, I guess they have things enough," Freddie replied. "You mean things like the old shawl and the piece of blanket, don't you, Flossie?"

"Yes, things like that. But I guess we took enough down."

Then Flossie and Freddie saw Bert hurrying into the garage.

"Oh, look!" whispered Freddie, pointing.

"He has bread and jam!" murmured Flossie.

"I didn't meant that," went on Freddie. "Dinah will give us some bread and jam if we ask. But there's Bert going in the garage and shutting the door. They must have something in there, for I saw Nan through the side window."

"I guess they have something in there," agreed Flossie. "Let's go and peek in!"

"Sure!" said her brother.

The two small twins walked softly toward the garage, but before they reached the place

Bert opened the door, looked out with some jam stains around his mouth, and said:

"You can't come in here."

"Why not?" asked Freddie.

"Because," retorted Bert, "I'm busy."

"Is Nan busy, too?" asked Flossie.

"Nan? Oh, yes, Nan is busy, too. Run along now. You can't come in here," and Bert moved to close the door.

"Why not?" asked Freddie again.

"Because," was all the answer Bert gave and then he slammed the door shut. The small twins stood there for a moment and then Flossie said:

"They have a secret in there, all right."

"Sure they have!" assented Freddie. "But I'm going to get Dinah to give me some bread and jam."

"So'm I," said Flossie.

As they turned away from the garage they could hear Bert and Nan talking inside the building. But if the talk was anything about a secret the small twins could not make out what it was. Anyhow, they were hungry.

"Bread an' jam!" exclaimed Dinah when they made their request in her kitchen a little later. "Suah, mah honey lambs! All de bread an' jam yo' all wants!"

She gave them generous slices, and while eating they forgot about the secret of Nan and Bert in the garage and almost forgot about their own secret in the cellar.

But suddenly Sam came in from out of doors and began looking around the room.

"Whut yo' want?" asked his wife.

"Where's mah ole shawl?" asked the colored chauffeur.

"Ole shawl?" repeated Dinah. Flossie and Freddie, with their slices of bread and jam half way to their mouths, paused in surprise.

"Yep! Dat ole shawl I brought in heah th' other day to hab yo' wash so's I could hab it ready to put on de car radiator when we got a freezin' spell. An' a freezin' spell is comin' soon, I reckon. I'll need dat ole shawl."

"Oh, dat ole shawl!" said Dinah, with a laugh. "Well, yo' can't hab dat, Sam!"

"I can't! Why not?"

" 'Cause I done use it."

"Yo' use my radiator shawl, Dinah? Whut fo'?"

"Nebber yo' mind, Sam Johnson!" she exclaimed, with a warning look at Flossie and Freddie. "I knows whut I's doin'. I'll git yo' suffin' else to put on de car. Dat ole shawl's needed fo' suffin' else. An' now yo' got to git outer mah kitchen! I's busy!"

"Oh—all right," answered Sam, meekly. When his wife talked that way he knew better than to stand in her way. "But I suah would like to know what yo' did wif dat ole shawl," he murmured as he walked out.

"Oh," whispered Flossie, as she went on eating her bread and jam, "sposin' he had gone down cellar and seen it?"

"Then we wouldn't have any secret," murmured Freddie.

"Don't worry, honey lambs!" chuckled Dinah. "I wouldn't let him go down."

By the time they had eaten their bread and jam and had played about in the front yard, Flossie and Freddie quite forgot about what Bert and Nan were doing in the garage. Once, as they ran close to the building in playing tag with Susie Larker and Harry Ford, the small Bobbsey twins heard the voices of Bert and Nan coming from the building. But what was said they could not make out.

For several days the Bobbsey twins kept close guard over their two secrets, Flossie and Freddie having theirs down cellar, and Bert and Nan theirs out in the garage. But it was Flossie and Freddie who were more anxious to discover the secret of Nan and Bert than the older twins were to find out why their small brother and sister went in and out of the cellar so often, with much whispering and giggling.

As for Bert and Nan, they did not seem to notice that Flossie and Freddie were closely watching them from day to day. Every afternoon when they came from school, Bert and Nan would slip into the garage. And if Freddie and his sister tried to follow they were told to go away. Once they didn't, and when Bert called his mother, Mrs. Bobbsey said to the small twins:

"It isn't nice to spy around and snoop, my dears. No matter what little game Nan and Bert are playing in the garage, you must not spy on them."

"Oh, is it a game?" asked Flossie.

"Sort of," admitted Nan.

"Could we play in it?" asked Freddie.

"Not now!" Bert said. "Just keep away. We'll tell you about it some day."

But this did not satisfy Flossie and Freddie. True, they did not spy any more too close to the garage. But once, when they saw Nan and Bert slip out and start down town, Freddie said:

"Let's trail 'em!"

"Trail 'em?" asked Flossie, wonderingly.

"Yes, like the Indians used to trail the white settlers," went on Freddie who had often played Wild West with his boy chums. "I mean, let's trail after Nan and Bert now and see where they go down town. Maybe we can find out the secret that way."

"Oh, let's!" agreed Flossie, always eager to have a part in anything Freddie did.

So when Bert and Nan went along the street, hurrying to get to the main section of the city of Lakeport known as "down town," they were trailed, or followed at a distance, by Flossie and Freddie.

"We'll watch and see where they go," whispered Flossie.

"Sure!" agreed her brother. "We'll find out their secret!"

CHAPTER VI

NAN'S ORANGE TIE

Bert and Nan Bobbsey were so much taken up by their talk as they hurried along the street, going down town, that they did not notice Freddie and Flossie trailing them.

It would have been quite easy for the older twins to have noticed the younger twins walking along after them, if Bert and Nan had taken the trouble to look behind them. For Flossie and Freddie, though the small boy had often played cowboy and Wild West, were not very good at taking the trail. They did not try to keep back out of sight of their brother and sister.

"Maybe they're only going down town to do some Christmas shopping, as Mother did the other day," suggested Flossie as she hurried along beside her twin brother.

"Maybe," agreed Freddie. "Anyhow, we'll find out."

They saw Bert and Nan turn a corner, and kept after them. At the corner was a large toy store and the double window was filled with Christmas presents. Bert and Nan stopped around the corner to look in one side of this window.

Peering through the other side of the window, which fronted on two streets, Freddie saw Bert and Nan looking in at the gifts just in time to stop. Otherwise he and Flossie might have run into the older twins, who would then have known that they were being trailed.

"What's the matter?" whispered Flossie as Freddie suddenly put out a hand and stopped her from turning the corner.

"Bert and Nan are right around the corner there, looking in the other side of this window!" Freddie whispered. "See!"

"Oh, yes!" murmured Flossie, and she drew back out of view. There was so much noise in the street from automobiles that neither Bert nor Nan heard the voices of their small brother and sister, and the older twins were so busy looking at the many toys in the window that they never thought of looking through the corner glass which, if they had done, would have given them a view of the small twin trailers.

Then, pressing as close against the window as they could, in company with other boys and girls also looking in, Freddie and Flossie heard Bert speak in rather loud tones to Nan. At the moment there was a lull in the street noises.

"Come on, Nan," said Bert. "We must hurry or he'll be gone."

"That's right," agreed Nan.

Freddie and Flossie wondered who "he" might be, and they wondered where Bert and Nan had to go in such a hurry.

Waiting until Bert and Nan got a little start, the small twins were soon once more trailing after them. Up one street and down another went Bert and Nan, and Freddie and Flossie followed as best they could. Luckily the small twins knew their way quite well all over "down town," so they did not get lost.

But a queer thing happened. They lost Bert and Nan. There was quite a lot of traffic on one street and when it had cleared away, Bert and Nan were not in sight.

"Oh, where are they?" murmured Flossie.

"I don't know," her brother answered. "They got away, I guess. They gave us the slip!"

"Oh, dear!" sighed Flossie. "That's too bad! Now we can't see where they go!"

"Maybe we can find 'em again," suggested Freddie, hopefully.

· But, though the two small twins looked here and there, up one street and down another, they did not again catch sight of Nan and Bert. Then, as it was getting late, Flossie and Freddie turned back toward their home.

"We'll follow 'em the next time they go down town," Freddie said.

"Yes, and then we'll find out their secret," agreed Flossie. "I wonder how our secret is?"

"Oh, all right, I guess," her brother answered. "We'll go down and look before supper."

"But we mustn't let Nan and Bert see us," cautioned the little blue-eyed girl.

"Oh, no!" Freddie replied.

What Nan and Bert did down town they did not speak of when they came home to supper. This was soon after Flossie and Freddie came tramping up from the cellar, following their return from their fruitless trailing errand. Bert and Nan well knew how to keep their secret.

But, for that matter, so did Flossie and Freddie. For though they went down cellar many times in the next two days, they watched their chances and did not enter the basement when anyone was around but Dinah.

"But you'll never tell, will you, Dinah?" asked Flossie.

"No, indeedy, honey lamb! I'll never tell!" promised the black cook.

The weather was getting colder now. It was only a few weeks before Christmas and the jolly excitement that always comes with the holidays began to be noticed about the Bobbsey home. It was hard to go to school those days, for there was so much else to think about besides lessons that it is a wonder any of the boys and girls could recite.

One day, when Freddie and Flossie were coming out of school a little ahead of their older brother and sister, Flossie would have run along home, as she generally did. But Freddie stopped her, saying:

"They're going down town again."

"Who?" asked Flossie.

"Bert and Nan. They're going right down from school. I heard Bert tell Nan so at recess."

"Oh!" murmured Flossie.

"And we can trail 'em!" added her small brother. "This time we won't lose 'em. We'll find out where they go and what the secret is."

"That'll be great!" agreed Flossie.

So the two small twins played about in the school yard until it was time for the older children to be dismissed. Then, hiding around the corner of the fence, Flossie and Freddie waited until they saw Bert and Nan hurrying off toward down town.

"Come on!" called Freddie, taking Flossie by the hand.

Once more the small twins were on the trail.

This time they had no trouble in keeping close behind Bert and Nan without being seen. The older twins hurried along, not even stopping to glance in store windows, though there were many fine things to look at. Flossie and Freddie did not get close enough to hear any talk. But it seemed very likely, from the businesslike way in which Bert and Nan hastened along, that they had an errand of some importance.

"We'll find out all about it now!" whispered Freddie.

"Sure!" murmured Flossie.

But once again the small twins were disappointed. Bert and Nan went along very sedately, and not at all as if they had any secret to hide. They walked toward a store and went inside when Flossie and Freddie were at the nearest corner.

"There they go!" Freddie exclaimed.

"I see 'em!" retorted Flossie.

"They've gone into that music store," went on Freddie.

"Let's look in," his twin sister suggested.

This they did, taking the risk of being seen by Nan and Bert. But the older Bobbsey children were talking to one of the clerks in the music store and did not see the "trailers" peering in.

"Pooh!" murmured Flossie as she saw Nan

with a sheet of music in her hand. "This isn't any secret."

"No, I guess it isn't," Freddie agreed. "Nan is just buying some new music for her piano lesson."

"And Bert is looking at a bugle," reported Flossie as the other Bobbsey boy walked about the store.

"Maybe he hopes he'll get one for Christmas," suggested Freddie. "A bugle horn would be nice, I think."

"I don't believe Mother would like it," said Flossie.

For a few moments they watched Nan and Bert in the music store. There did not seem to be any secret about the visit. Then, when Flossie saw Nan hand back the sheet of music to the clerk and start out toward the front door, the little girl called:

"Come on, Freddie, before they catch us!"

"All right!" he answered. "All our work for nothing!" he sighed as they ran on ahead to get home before Nan and Bert.

"Maybe they haven't any secret after all," said Flossie.

"Oh, yes, they have a secret all right," decided Freddie. "And I'm going to find out what it is."

"Then I'll help you!" offered Flossie.

But as several days passed, and Bert and Nan, though going out to the garage several times, showed no unusual signs of having a secret, Flossie began to have her doubts. But Freddie did not.

"I tell you they have a secret!" he said earnestly.

"How do you know?" asked Flossie.

"Because," replied Freddie, "yesterday, when they went in the garage I heard Nan say it was her turn to yell out loud now."

"What did she mean—yell out loud?" asked Flossie.

"I don't know. That's part of the secret," was Freddie's reply.

"Did you listen to hear what they yelled about in the garage?"

"I tried to, Flossie, but Bert came out and made me go away. I wish I knew what their secret was."

"So do I. But, anyhow, ours is all right down cellar."

"Yes, and it's a wonderful secret, too!"

"Just wonderful!" said Flossie, her blue eyes shining.

A few days after this Bert and Nan again slipped off down town. Before they went they talked for some time back of the garage, and Flossie and Freddie heard several things said that made them wonder very much.

But this time when the two small twins started to follow the older ones down town, Nan discovered the trick and made Flossie and Freddie go back.

"If you don't, I'll call Mother!" Nan threatened.

"Oh, all right! What do we care?" said Flossie, turning up her little nose.

"Ha! Ha!" laughed Nan. "Don't you wish you could find out?"

"No, we don't!" declared Freddie, "Anyhow, we have a secret of our own, so there!"

But Bert and Nan hurried off down the street, paying no more heed to the small twins who were left to themselves. They did not dare trail Nan and Bert now, for fear of being found out.

"Let's go down cellar," proposed Freddie.

"Oh, sure!" agreed Flossie.

So they went down to look at the secret, and while they were there Freddie had a sudden idea.

"I'm going up and get something," he said to Flossie.

"What for?" Flossie wanted to know.

"So it will look more stylish." was the answer.

"What will look more stylish?"

"Why, it!"

"What'll you get?" Flossie wanted to know, though she had not found out what "it" was.

"Oh, something," was all Freddie answered.

And when he came down with "something," Flossie clapped her hands in delight and said:

"Oh, that's pretty!"

"That's what I thought," said Freddie. "Will you help me put it on, Flossie?"

The little girl said she would, but just then her mother called her.

"Oh, I've got to run up!" gasped Flossie. "If mother comes down here. she'll find out the secret."

"Hurry up then," advised Freddie. "We

don't want her to see. I guess I can put it on myself."

Flossie hurried up from the cellar before her mother reached the kitchen in her search for the little girl, who was wanted to try on a new dress just being finished. So Freddie was left alone with the secret. Mrs. Bobbsey was so much occupied with seeing that Flossie's dress fitted that the mother of the twins did not think to ask where Flossie had been.

It was the day after this that, hurrying out of her room where she had been dressing to go on a late afternoon shopping trip with her mother, Nan called:

"Has anyone seen my new orange tie?"

"Isn't it on your bureau?" her mother asked.

"No, it isn't," replied Nan. "Oh, my lovely orange tie is gone and I wanted to wear it with this new blouse! Where is my orange tie?"

Down in the hall, Flossie heard this.

"Oh!" murmured Flossie.

She looked for her brother Freddie, but he was not to be seen.

CHAPTER VII

FREDDIE'S MISTAKE

Nan Bobbsey was hurrying around her room, opening one drawer after another in the search for her orange-colored tie.

"It's very queer where it went," Flossie heard Nan say. "I'm sure I left it on my bureau."

"Well, don't upset everything while you are looking for it, Nan," warned Mrs. Bobbsey. "Search carefully. I'll come up and help you in a moment. But wouldn't it be better to wear some other tie instead of losing time looking for the orange one?"

"No, Mother, thank you, but it wouldn't," said Nan, and her voice showed that she was much disappointed. "I want that tie, for it's the only one that matches this blouse. Oh, dear! Where is it?"

"Flossie, you go up and help Nan look,"

suggested Mrs. Bobbsey. "I'll be up in just a moment, after I telephone. Run along up, Flossie."

"All right, Mother," came the answer. Flossie started up the stairs but there was a strange look on her face, and more than once she glanced down the hall to see if Freddie was there. But he wasn't.

"Oh, dear!" sighed Flossie to herself. "I wish he'd come It's all his fault!"

When Flossie entered the room Nan was still moving quickly about, looking here and there for the missing tie. Either Nan suspected something or the look on Flossie's face told her something. For no sooner had Flossie entered than Nan cried out:

"Flossie Bobbsey, did you take my orange tie?"

For a moment Flossie was so surprised and frightened (just a little bit) that she could not answer. She stood there with her mouth open, all ready for words to come out, but none came.

"Did you?" repeated Nan.

Then Flossie found her voice and murmured:

"No—no, Nan, I—I didn't take your tie."

"Honest?" insisted Nan.

"Honest! Cross my heart!" exclaimed Flossie.

"Oh, you needn't do that!" retorted Nan. "But somebody took my orange tie and I want it! If you did take it, Flossie, or know where it is and will give it back to me, I'll forgive you."

"Honest, Nan, I didn't take it. But maybe——"

Just then Mrs. Bobbsey came upstairs and Flossie did not finish what she had started to say.

"Did you find it?" asked Nan's mother.

"No, I didn't," Nan answered sorrowfully.

"I thought, from the way I heard you and Flossie talking," went on Mrs. Bobbsey. "that perhaps——"

She paused and looked at her little girl.

"I was just asking Flossie if she took my tie," explained Nan. "But she said she didn't."

"Really I didn't!" burst out Flossie.

"And Flossie always tells the truth," put in Mrs. Bobbsey. "But perhaps you know, my dear," she went on, once more turning to the little twin, "where Nan's orange tie is."

However, Flossie had not stayed to hear the last of what her mother was saying. Holding her hand over her mouth lest perhaps words might come out that she did not intend, the little girl hurried down the stairs.

Nan and her mother looked at each other curiously.

"Did you see that?" murmured Nan. "She ran away!"

"Yes," agreed Mrs. Bobbsey. "I can't imagine what has gotten into the child."

"She knows something about my orange tie!" decided Nan.

"Do you think so?"

"I'm sure of it! She didn't take it herself, but she knows who did. That's why she hurried out of the room before we could ask her, for of course she would tell the truth."

"Yes, of course. But do you think Bert— Oh, no, he wouldn't do such a thing. Before we say anything more, Nan, let's you and me have a good look around the room. We may find that the tie has fallen off back of your bureau."

"I looked on the floor, Mother."

"Well, it may be caught back of the bureau. I'll pull it out."

Meanwhile Flossie was hurrying out to a little house, a sort of tool shed, where Sam Johnson kept rakes, shovels, and hoes that he used on the garden in summer. The tools were now put away, but Flossie and Freddie kept their sleds in this shack and Freddie had said he was going to polish the runners of his sled.

"Because, pretty soon, it's going to snow," Freddie had said.

Flossie remembered this when she wanted to find her twin brother, and she now hurried to the small house. From inside it came a scraping sound and, looking in, Flossie saw Freddie rubbing some sandpaper on the rusty, steel runners of his sled.

"I'll polish yours as soon as I have finished," Freddie said when he saw Flossie.

"Oh, Freddie," gasped his sister, "something terrible has happened!"

"What!" he cried, jumping up and knocking his sled aside. "Did Bert find out about our secret?"

"No, he didn't find out, but this is about our secret all the same."

"What do you mean?" asked Freddie, wiping some of the rust off his hands onto his knickers.

"Nan's orange tie!" exclaimed Flossie, solemnly. "She's found out it's gone off her bureau."

"Nan's—orange—tie!" repeated Freddie, slowly.

"Yes," went on Flossie, shaking a little, chubby finger at her brother. "Nan's orange tie! She's looking all over for it and at first she thought I'd taken it. I said I hadn't, but I ran out before she could ask me any more questions."

"Oh, that old orange tie!" murmured Freddie. "Pooh, that's nothing!"

"Yes, it is something!" insisted Flossie. "And it isn't an *old* tie, Freddie. It's Nan's *new* one and I saw you take it down cellar. That's why I ran out of the room before they could ask me. You did take it down cellar, didn't you?"

"I took an old piece of orange ribbon off

Nan's bureau and carried it down cellar," Freddie admitted. "Sure!"

"It wasn't an old ribbon," said Flossie. "It was Nan's best, new tie."

"Then," said Freddie slowly, as he wiped more rust off his hands, "I guess I made a sort of mistake."

"I guess you did!" agreed Flossie. "What did you want of it, anyhow?"

"Well," resumed Freddie, "I sort of thought that yellow ribbon would look nice on the basket—you know—the basket."

"Yes," agreed Flossie, "I know—the basket. Did you put Nan's tie on it?"

"Right on the handle," stated the small boy. "It looks nice, too!"

"Well, you'd better go right down cellar and take it off!" warned Flossie. "Mother and Nan will be out here pretty soon, looking for you, I guess, and if you take the tie back first, it will be better."

"I guess it will," Freddie agreed. "Golly! I didn't think that old piece of yellow ribbon was any good. And it looked awfully nice tied on the handle of the basket, Flossie."

"Yes, I s'pose it did. But we'll have to get

something else," said the little girl. "Hurry now! I think I hear Mother and Nan coming! Run!"

Freddie ran, going down cellar by the outside door just as Nan and her mother, who had decided to follow Flossie, came out into the yard. Both Mrs. Bobbsey and Nan were suspicious of the way in which Flossie had acted—running away in that fashion.

"Oh, here you are, Flossie," remarked Mrs. Bobbsey as her little daughter came out of the tool shed.

"Yes'm, I'm here," said Flossie, demurely.

"Where's Freddie?" asked Nan who, as she said later, had begun to guess what had happened.

Before Flossie could answer Freddie came up out of the cellar carrying the lost orange tie.

"Oh, there's my new tie!" cried Nan in delight. "Where did you get it, Freddie? Oh, don't wrinkle it!" she cried as she noticed how carelessly Freddie was handling the strip of silk. "And your hands are so dirty!"

"That isn't dirt!" declared Freddie. "It's just rust off my sled runners."

"Oh, but it might get on my lovely tie!" cried Nan, quickly, taking it from him. "Where did you get it and what were you doing with it, Freddie Bobbsey?"

"I took it off your bureau this morning," Freddie answered. "I thought it was an old one and you wouldn't care."

"Oh, my best, new tie!" exclaimed Nan. "As if I wouldn't care! Oh, Freddie Bobbsey! Anyhow, what did you want of it?"

Freddie looked at Flossie and Flossie looked at Freddie.

"What were you doing with my orange tie?" repeated Nan.

Just then Freddie gave a loud cry and rushed toward the cellar.

"Come on, Flossie!" he yelled. "Don't let him get in! Don't let him get in!"

CHAPTER VIII

STRANGE VOICES

FLOSSIE BOBBSEY made as quick a dash for the open cellar door as did her brother Freddie. With both the small twins running and shouting there was so much excitement that Nan forgot all about the question she had asked Freddie, as to why he took her orange tie.

"What's the matter?" asked Mrs. Bobbsey, for she had her back turned toward the cellar door for the moment.

"It's a strange dog and he's going in!" yelled Freddie.

"We mustn't let him!" shrieked Flossie. "Get away from there!" she cried.

Nan and her mother now saw what had caused all the excitement. A large, black dog, a strange one in the neighborhood, had come into the yard and had started for the open cellar. Flossie and Freddie had very good reasons for not wanting a dog to go down where they had their mysterious secret.

Dinah, who was busy in the kitchen, heard the shouts of Flossie and Freddie, the surprised exclamations of Nan and Mrs. Bobbsey, and the barking of the strange dog. Then Dinah acted quickly.

Catching up a broom, she hurried out and down the back steps, moving more quickly than one would have thought such a fat person could do. Dinah got to the cellar steps just as the black animal was slipping toward the open door.

"No yo' don't!" cried the jolly, black cook. "Dish yeah ain't yo' cellar an' yo' cain't go down! Yo' got to git right away! Shoo! Shoo!"

"Dinah must think the dog is a chicken!" said Nan with a little laugh. "She's shooing him!"

"She certainly came out quickly enough," remarked Mrs. Bobbsey.

With a swoop of her broom, Dinah sent the strange dog scurrying away before Flossie and Freddie could get near enough to do anything. They had picked up some pebbles to throw at the black creature. But they loved animals and would not hurt even a stray dog.

"But just little stones wouldn't have hurt him," Freddie explained afterward. "They would only tickle him and make him run away."

"Yes," agreed Flossie.

But Freddie didn't have to throw any stones, for Dinah drove the dog away with her broom and the cellar secret was safe.

Flossie and Freddie breathed easier. They were somewhat afraid lest their mother or Nan ask them why they didn't want the strange dog to go down cellar, but Dinah took this explanation upon herself.

"I didn't want no strange beast gwine in among all mah canned fruit," she said. It was true that Dinah had many glass jars of fruit in the cellar.

"Indeed, it's a good thing the dog didn't get down there," agreed Mrs. Bobbsey. "He might have broken some."

"You saw that dog just in time, Freddie," said Nan, smoothing out her orange tie and making sure it wasn't soiled and that her small brother had not put any rust on it.

"Yes, I saw him," Freddie answered.

"I wonder whose dog it is?" asked Mrs. Bobbsey.

"I never saw him before," Flossie stated.

"Neither did I," Freddie added. "Anyhow, he's gone."

"Ef he hadn't gone I'd breshed him hard wif mah broom!" murmured Dinah as she went back to her kitchen. As she did so she gave Flossie and Freddie a look which Nan and her mother did not notice. It was as if Dinah had said to the small twins:

"Don't worry. Your secret is still safe. But if that dog had gone down cellar it might have been discovered."

Flossie and Freddie were very glad the dog had not gotten in where they had their secret hidden.

The excitement made Nan forget all about asking Freddie what use he had made of her orange tie. Nan had not heard Freddie tell Flossie about fastening the bow of orange ribbon on the handle of some basket. If Nan had heard that she might have been much puzzled.

"You mustn't take any more ribbons or

anything else off my bureau, Freddie," Nan said to him as she went in to get dressed to go out with her girl chums.

"No, I won't," Freddie promised. "I wouldn't have taken this one, only I thought it was old and you didn't want it."

"Well, I'll forgive you this time," Nan said.

Then, fearing Nan might ask him more questions, Freddie called to his other sister:

"Come on, Flossie! You can help me sand-paper the sled runners. It may snow pretty soon and then we'll be ready to coast down-hill."

"Oh, what fun that'll be!" cried Flossie.

With Nan going out, wearing her new orange tie and the blouse to match, with Bert off having fun with some of his boy chums, Flossie and Freddie now had the place to themselves. As they were going toward the tool house where their sleds were kept, Freddie said:

"Let's look in the garage and see if we can find their secret."

"Whose secret?" Flossie wanted to know.

"The one Nan and Bert have in there."

"Oh, yes, let's!" cried the little girl. "We can fix the sleds after a while."

But their search around the garage was useless. They looked in nooks and corners, under the car, in it, and in the closets where Sam kept his cleaning cloths, oils, and greases. Nothing like a secret was to be seen.

"Maybe they took it away," suggested Flossie.

"Maybe," agreed Freddie. "Anyhow, our secret is all right in the cellar, isn't it?"

"Yes," his sister replied. "But if that dog had gotten in maybe it wouldn't be."

"We'll have to keep that outside door closed," decided Freddie.

Not having found anything about the secret of Nan and Bert in the garage, Flossie and Freddie went back to work on the sleds. In a short time Freddie had rubbed most of the rust off the runners of his snow glider and then he began on Flossie's.

"Yours is rustier than mine was," he said as he began rubbing.

"Do you want me to help rub it off?" asked Flossie. "If you have any more sandpaper I'll help."

"No, you'd better not," decided her brother. "It gets all over your hands. Look!"

He held up his hands which were a reddish yellow from the rust that had come off the sled runners.

"Oh, you look so funny!" laughed Flossie.

"Pooh! It'll wash off!" answered Freddie as he rubbed, making more red rust dust.

He finished Flossie's sled and was looking over the runners to make sure he had left no rough spots which would hold the coaster back on a snow-covered hill, when, all of a sudden, Sam Johnson, who had been down town, came past the little tool shed. The colored man gave one look at Freddie's yellowish-red hands and shouted:

"Oh, mah goodness! Accident! Yo' suah is bad hurt, boy! I'll carry you in the house!"

Catching Freddie up in his arms, Sam made a dash for the kitchen, shouting as he ran:

"Dinah! Dinah! Git a basin ob water! Freddie's hurt!"

"No, I'm not hurt! I'm not!" yelled Freddie, laughing and trying to scramble out of Sam's arms. "I'm all right. It's only rust!"

"Yes, I guess suffin' did bust!" said Sam, who, in his excitement, did not hear just right. "But Dinah'll take keer ob yo'. Don't be afeerd!"

"Put him down! He isn't hurt!" shouted Flossie, running after Sam and her brother.

By this time Dinah, hearing her husband's shouts, had looked out of the kitchen door and, seeing Sam running up with the little boy in his arms and catching a glance of his yellow hands, guessed that something dreadful had happened.

"Oh, mah po' honey lamb!" murmured the black cook as she held the door open for Sam to come in. "Who done it?"

"Nobody did anything!" shouted Freddie as he was set on his feet. He was laughing hard.

"Nobody did nuffin'!" cried Sam. "Whut yo' mean? Look at yo' hands, Freddie!"

He pointed to the reddish stains and then, amid laughter, Freddie said:

"That's only rust off my sled runners. I cleaned my sled and Flossie's so we'd be ready when it snows."

"Only rust?" repeated Sam, wonderingly,

As he looked at Freddie's hands. "Why, so 'tis!" he went on as he rubbed a little off. "Jes' rust! I suah did think dat yo' was bad hurt, Freddie. Dat's why I kotched yo' up so quick an' run yo' into de house."

"Hu! Jes' like Sam Johnson to think rust was suffin' else!" said Dinah with a laugh. "Go 'long wif yo' now!"

"But it was very kind of Sam to act so quickly when he thought Freddie was hurt," said Mrs. Bobbsey, coming into the kitchen to see what all the excitement was about. "It was very good of you, Sam."

"Oh, Sam's good!" chuckled Dinah. "I'll never say he ain't! But he can't see straight! Ha! Ha! Ha!"

"I kin see as straight as you!" chuckled her husband.

He went out to the garage, Freddie calling after him:

"Well, anyhow, Sam, thanks for giving me such a funny ride!"

"Ha! Ha! It was funny!" chuckled black Sam. "But I suah am glad yo' isn't hurt!"

"My goodness! What dirty hands!" murmured Mrs. Bobbsey. "You must wash them down here, Freddie. I can't have you staining up the basin in the bathroom. Dinah, get him some old cloths to dry on. That rust will never come out of a towel."

" 'Deed it won't, ma'am. Heah, Freddie, let Dinah scrub you up."

"How did you ever get so dirty?" asked his mother as the water and soap began to be used.

"Off the sled runners," said Freddie, cheerfully. "But they're all fixed now, and I won't have to sandpaper 'em until next year."

"I'm glad of that," his mother remarked with a laugh.

It was two or three days after this that Freddie and Flossie were out in the yard anxiously peering up at the sky.

"Do you think it looks like snow?" asked Flossie.

"I think it does, a little," Freddie answered. "I hope it snows a lot tonight, so tomorrow we can go coasting."

"Oh, what fun!" murmured Flossie.

The two small twins were walking toward the garage when, all of a sudden, they heard strange voices coming from the place. Loud voices they were, too; voices that seemed to be raised in anger.

Flossie and Freddie looked at each other in surprise.

CHAPTER IX

LOCKED IN

"WHAT—what you s'pose it is?" whispered Flossie.

"Sh! Listen!" warned her brother.

"They're in our garage, aren't they?"

"Sure they are!" said Freddie.

There was no doubt of it. The small twins were near the building where Sam kept the car, and the voices were coming from the garage. Even with the doors and windows closed, on account of the cold weather, Freddie and Flossie could hear the loud talk.

"I tell you it can't be done!" shouted some one.

"That was Nan! I'm sure of it!" whispered Flossie.

"Yes, it sounded like her," agreed Freddie.

They kept still, not far from the back windows of the place, and listened carefully.

"I tell you it must be done!" bawled another voice.

"That was Bert," said Freddie.

"Yes," agreed his twin sister, "it was."

Then, once again, Nan's voice, raised as if in anger, shouted:

"Well, I'm not going to do it!"

Flossie and Freddie looked at each other not only in some alarm, but also in surprise.

"Oh! Oh, this is terrible!" roared Bert.

For a moment Flossie and Freddie listened. The voices in the garage died away into murmurs, so the two small twins could not hear what was said. Then, once more they broke out as Bert yelled:

"This is enough! It's too much! I'll fix you for this!"

"Go on! I dare you to!" shouted back Nan.

"Oh, oh!" sorrowfully murmured Flossie. "How terrible! Bert and Nan must be having a fight!"

"It sounds so," agreed Freddie. "They're quarreling about something, I guess."

"Had we better go tell Mother?" asked Flossie.

Freddie hesitated. Telling, or carrying tales,

was not what the Bobbsey twins very often did. Their father had told them never to do this. But Nan and Bert so seldom quarreled —hardly ever, in fact—that when they did, it made everything different.

"I'm going to tell Mother!" suddenly decided Flossie.

"No, don't!" begged Freddie. "Daddy says telling isn't fair. Maybe we had better go in and tell Nan and Bert to stop fighting."

"I don't guess they're zactly fighting," observed Flossie.

"Well, quarreling, then. We'd better tell them to stop."

"Come on!" agreed Flossie.

But before the small twins could carry out their plans the garage door opened and Bert looked out. He seemed surprised to see Flossie and Freddie coming around the corner of the garage.

"Hello!" he exclaimed. "What are you two doing around here?"

"Noth—nothing," answered Freddie slowly.

"Well, you'd better run away," went on Bert, kindly enough. "Nan and I are busy in here and we can't be bothered. You run away now and I'll take you for a walk in a little while."

"Oh, will you?" cried Flossie eagerly, quickly beginning to forget about the quarrel she and Freddie had heard.

"Down town?" asked Freddie.

"Yes, down town," promised Bert. "I'll treat you to ice cream soda, too."

"Oh, golly gosh! That will be fine!" cried Freddie.

"Just lovely!" echoed Flossie.

"Then run away now."

For a moment Flossie and Freddie hesitated. They wanted, very much, to ask what was the meaning of the loud voices, but after Bert had promised them a treat, it did not seem to be just the right thing to do. Perhaps, after all, everything was all right. Bert was smiling and when the small twins had a glimpse of Nan through a window she was also smiling. So the quarrel, whatever it might be about, did not seem to be very serious.

"Hop along now," Bert urged. "And don't come back around the garage any more. Nan and I have something to do. If I catch you here again—no ice cream soda!"

This threat was enough to make Freddie and Flossie promise not to come near the place. So they walked away while Bert went back in the garage and closed the door. Then the two small twins once more heard the murmur of his voice and Nan's.

"What do you s'pose they're doing?" asked the little girl.

"I don't know," confessed Freddie. "But, anyhow, it isn't much, I guess. And maybe we can find out the secret down town."

"How can we do that?" Flossie wanted to know.

"Well," replied her brother, "Bert is going to take us down town for a walk to get ice cream sodas, isn't he?"

"Yes," Flossie admitted.

"And every once in a while Nan and Bert slip off by themselves down town to do something, don't they?"

"Oh, yes. And we followed 'em but we couldn't find out anything," Flossie agreed.

"Well, maybe we'll find out *this time*," said her brother. "I'm going to keep my eyes open."

"So'll I."

The smaller twins kept their promise not to go near the garage again, and after a while Nan and Bert came out, laughing and talking together in low voices as if they had never exchanged harsh words.

"It's very queer," sighed Flossie.

"Very queer!" agreed her small brother.

"Come on now!" invited Bert. "All aboard for ice cream soda!"

"Oh, goodie!" cried Flossie and Freddie.

"Do you think it will be all right to take them?" asked Nan.

"Sure!" Bert answered. "But you can go tell Mother about it if you like."

"I think it would be better," Nan said as she hurried into the house. She came back in a few moments to say that Mrs. Bobbsey had given permission for the four twins to go down town.

"But we must be home in time for supper," Nan said.

"Oh, sure! I wouldn't miss supper!" chuckled Bert. "We're going to have chicken!"

"Oh, goodie!" cried Flossie and Freddie again. This certainly was a day of surprises.

For a time, so delighted were the small twins to go down town with Bert and Nan with the promise of wonderful ice cream sodas in the big drug store, that neither Flossie nor Freddie thought about the strange actions of the older twins in the garage. They all looked in the store windows which were beginning to be filled with Christmas presents, and this sight-seeing was so delightful that Flossie and Freddie could hardly be dragged away from one large toy shop.

"I just want to look some more at that fire engine," Freddie said, pointing to a red one with a rubber hose, something like his own toy. "I want to see if it's bigger than mine."

"Well, it isn't, I can tell you that," said Nan with a laugh.

"And if you don't hurry along all the ice cream may melt," stated Bert with a mirthful chuckle.

"Oh, come on!" Freddie then urged.

"Wait! Wait!" cried Flossie. "I want to look at that doll again!"

But the two small twins were finally made to leave the toy store windows and they followed the older ones to the drug store where Nan had an errand to do for her mother, and where the ice cream sodas were also to be had.

It took Flossie and Freddie some little time to make up their minds whether they would have vanilla, strawberry, pineapple or chocolate, but at length Freddie, after first choosing vanilla, switched to chocolate. And Flossie, after first deciding that she wanted pineapple also decided that she, too, would have chocolate.

"Now, don't spill any of it," warned Bert as the soda clerk pushed the tall, foaming glasses toward the small twins.

"Don't worry!" laughed Freddie. "It's too good to spill!"

"It sure is!" agreed Flossie.

Bert and Nan also had sodas, but they finished theirs first. The small twins always ate their treats slowly to make them last longer. Then Nan went to the drug counter to get something for her mother, and Bert, pushing away his empty glass, said to Flossie and Freddie:

"I'm just going across the street for a few

minutes. You wait here with Nan after you finish your sodas."

"All right," answered Freddie. Flossie didn't say anything, as she had her mouth full of chocolate ice cream.

Then Freddie, having scraped out of his glass all there was to eat or drink, got down off the stool and went to the big, front window of the drug store. He looked at Nan talking to the clerk at the drug counter, and then Freddie looked across the street. He saw Bert going in the same music store where, once before, the small twins had noticed Nan and Bert entering.

"I wonder what Bert is going in there for?" mused Freddie. And when a little later Nan, having finished her purchase, came over to stand beside him, Freddie asked:

"What did Bert go in that music store for?"

"Oh, did he go in there?" asked Nan with a smile.

"Yes, he did," said Freddie as Flossie, having now finished her soda, came over to join them.

"And we saw you go in there with Bert the other day," went on Flossie.

"Oh, did you?" asked Nan, calmly. "Well, what of it?"

"Is it a secret?" asked Freddie, eagerly.

"Little boys shouldn't ask questions!" retorted Nan. "Now you have had a fine treat, Freddie, you and Flossie, so you must be good and not talk too much nor ask too many questions."

For a moment Freddie looked at Nan's smiling face. He wanted to ask many questions, not only as to why Bert went into the music store, but also about the loud voices in the garage.

"It's too near Christmas for little boys and girls to ask many questions," went on Nan, still smiling.

"Oh, all right!" exclaimed Freddie. "Then I won't. But Flossie and I have a secret, too."

"Have you?" asked Nan, but she did not show much interest. "Well, that's nice. But don't speak to Bert about going in that store. He might not like it."

"All right," Flossie agreed as Freddie nodded his head.

Bert came back a little later, whistling, and when he looked at Nan he said:

"Everything is all right."

"That's good," she said.

Going home along the streets lined by more stores, the windows of which were filled with Christmas toys, so took the minds of Flossie and Freddie off everything else that they gave hardly a thought to the strange actions of Nan and Bert.

"Anyhow, I guess they can have a secret the same as we can," said Freddie to his little sister that night.

"Sure!" she agreed. They had been down in the cellar to look at their own secret, slipping into the basement when Dinah gave them word that the coast was clear. Neither Mr. nor Mrs. Bobbsey, Nan nor Bert, saw the small twins go down and come up.

Their secret was still safe.

So the days went on. The weather grew colder, Christmas was coming nearer, and once there was a little flurry of snow. This set Flossie and Freddie wild with delight and made them eager to get out their sleds. But the snow did not last long.

"But there will be more." their mother told them

There was so much Christmas excitement around the Bobbsey home that even Nan and Bert felt it rather hard to go to school. However, the holidays would soon arrive and for two weeks or more there would be no classes.

One Friday afternoon when the class of Flossie and Freddie was about to be dismissed, Miss Trent, the teacher, asked:

"Who wants to remain and help me clean off the blackboards?"

Many hands were raised, but the teacher selected Flossie and Freddie Bobbsey. The small twins were quite proud to be allowed to stay in to help their teacher, and soon they were busy cleaning the boards on one side of the room, while Miss Trent did those on the other.

Then another teacher came in to say that Miss Trent was wanted down in the principal's office, and, turning to the twins, she said:

"You needn't stay any longer, my dears. Thank you very much. I can finish the boards. Run along."

She hurried out of the room, but Flossie said:

"Let's surprise her. Let's stay in and do all the boards. We can do it before she gets back."

"Sure!" agreed Freddie.

They brushed away at the chalk marks until all the boards were clean. Then, as Miss Trent had not returned, they put on their hats and coats to leave. But when Freddie tried the door it would not open.

"Golly, Flossie!" he exclaimed. "We're locked in!"

CHAPTER X

WINTER FUN

FLOSSIE BOBBSEY was so busy at that moment brushing off a little chalk mark in the lower corner of a blackboard where she had missed it, that she did not quite hear what Freddie said. After wiping off that last bit of chalk, using her cap, for she had put away the erasers, Flossie asked:

"What's the matter, Freddie?"

"Lots is the matter!" exclaimed the little boy, tugging at the door. "We're locked in!"

"Locked in?" cried Flossie, in surprise. "Why, that can't be! Miss Trent just went out of the door and it wasn't locked then."

"Well, it's locked now," went on Freddie. "Just you try it."

Flossie tried. She could not open the door.

"It really is locked," she said in a low voice.

"That's what I told you," went on her

brother. "We're locked in all right. How are we going to get out?"

Flossie looked around the room. There was another door besides the one which the children had tried in vain to open. With a little exclamation of joy Flossie ran toward this. But she had forgotten that this door led only into Miss Borden's room, back of Miss Trent's, and it did not take Flossie long to find out that the door leading from Miss Borden's room to the hall was also locked.

"We can't get out that way," said Flossie to Freddie.

"No," he agreed. "But maybe we can get out of a window."

There were several windows in each room, but they were rather high from the ground outside, as Flossie and Freddie knew. Besides, all the windows were locked and the catch was very high up on the sash. Neither of the small twins could reach the window-lock without a step ladder, and there was none to be had.

"What are we going to do?" asked Flossie in a low voice as she saw the day beginning to darken. Days are short in December. The sun goes to bed early and it soon gets dark.

The little twins had stayed in for some time to help clean the blackboards, and it was getting dark rather quickly now. "What are we going to do?" asked Flossie once more.

"If I could only open one of these doors," murmured Freddie, again trying the one in Miss Trent's room and then the one in Miss Borden's. But both were locked fast. "If I had a buttonhook maybe I could unlock one of the doors," went on Freddie.

"What do you mean—with a buttonhook?" asked Flossie.

"Once, when our garage got locked and Bert couldn't find the key," explained the little boy, "he opened it with a buttonhook and I saw him. Bert put the buttonhook in the lock and turned it just as if it was a key. So if I had a buttonhook now maybe I could open this door."

"But you haven't a buttonhook, have you?" asked Flossie.

"No, I haven't," replied her brother. "Have you?"

Flossie shook her head, adding:

"I haven't any pockets, like you."

"That's so." Freddie admitted. "But I

haven't a buttonhook in any of my pockets. I have a fishhook, though!" he exclaimed with delight as his searching fingers found one stuck in a cork so it would not scratch him. How long the fishhook had been in his pocket Freddie did not know. He had not been fishing for some time. Cold weather is no time to catch fish, unless you wait until some pond freezes and then cut a hole through the ice. It was not yet cold enough for that.

"You'd better be careful about that fishhook," warned Flossie. "You can't open a locked door with it, I don't believe, and it might stick in your fingers."

"Yes, that's so," admitted Freddie. "A buttonhook won't stick you, but I haven't one. I wonder how we got locked in, anyhow?"

The children thought back over what had happened. They had been helping Miss Trent clean the boards when she had been called to the principal's office. She had told them that they had better run along home, but Freddie and Flossie wanted to stay and finish cleaning the boards. Miss Trent had not come back and when the twins wanted to go out they couldn't.

"I guess the janitor came along and locked the door," said Flossie.

"I guess so," agreed Freddie. "He didn't think we were in here."

"Why didn't Miss Trent tell him?" Flossie wanted to know.

"Maybe she didn't see him, or maybe she went home and forgot all about us," suggested Freddie.

"Maybe," and Flossie sighed. "But, Freddie, what are we going to do?" she went on. "It'll be really dark soon. I don't want to stay here all night."

"I don't, either," agreed the little boy. "Oh, if I only had a buttonhook!"

"Maybe there's one in Miss Trent's desk," suggested Flossie. "She sometimes takes things, like buttonhooks, away from the boys in our class when they're playing with 'em instead of studying. And then she puts 'em in her desk. I mean, she puts the buttonhooks in her desk."

"Ho! Ho!" laughed Freddie. "I guess she couldn't put a *boy* in her desk."

"No," agreed Flossie. "she couldn't. But

maybe we can find a buttonhook that way
and you can open the door with it."

However, Miss Trent's desk, up on the platform in the front of the room, was locked.
And so was Miss Borden's. But when Freddie went in Miss Borden's room to continue
his search, Flossie saw something that made
her give a cry of joy.

"Oh, look!" she shouted, pointing.

"What?" asked Freddie.

"That bell!" went on his sister, showing
him one on a shelf in the corner of the room.
"That's the bell Miss Borden rings out of the
window when she wants her children to come
in from their recess, which is different from
ours." Miss Borden had the kindergarten
children. When they went out in the yard to
play, at a different hour from that of the other
classes, their teacher summoned her pupils
back into the room by ringing a large hand-
bell out of the window. There was no need to
ring the big bell which summoned the older
children back from their recess play.

"Ring that bell, Freddie!" exclaimed his
sister. "Somebody will hear us and let us out."

"But there aren't any windows open."

"No matter!" said Flossie. "Ring it, anyhow! Ring it loud."

Freddie picked up the hand-bell and began to clang it as loudly as he could. It made a great noise in the closed room, and Flossie held her hands over her ears. Louder and louder Freddie rang the bell.

"Stop! Stop!" cried Flossie, after a while.

"Why, is anybody coming?" Freddie wanted to know.

"I don't know. But if anybody did come we couldn't hear 'em with all that noise you're making."

"Well, you told me to ring it loud," said Freddie.

"Yes, ring it loud, and then wait a little to see if somebody is coming. It would be better if a window was open," went on Flossie. "Then maybe a policeman out in the street would hear it and he would break open the door."

"Firemen are better for breaking doors than policemen," said Freddie. "I'm going to be a fireman when I grow up."

"Well, I don't care if a policeman or a fireman breaks open the door so long as we get out," sighed Flossie. "It's getting dark, Freddie. Ring the bell again! Ring it hard!"

Freddie did, making the room echo with the clanging. Then, all of a sudden, voices were heard shouting out in the hall.

"Who is in there? What's the matter? Who are you?"

"Flossie and Freddie Bobbsey!" shouted the little boy, as he put the bell back on the shelf and ran to the door. "We're locked in!"

There was the rattle of a key in the lock. The door was swung open, and in the hall stood the janitor, the principal, and Miss Trent.

"Oh, Flossie and Freddie!" cried their teacher. "Oh, you poor darlings! To be locked in! But when I left you in my room I told you to go home!"

"Yes'm, I know," said Freddie. "But we didn't like to go without cleaning all the boards."

"That was good of you," murmured Miss Trent.

"And then, after you'd gone out and we'd finished the boards and we wanted to go home, we couldn't," explained Flossie.

"I came along and locked the doors," stated the janitor. "I didn't know anybody was left in the rooms."

"And I supposed that Freddie and Flossie had gone home, or I would have told you," said the teacher. "Oh, I'm so sorry about this! You poor children!"

"Oh, I wasn't afraid," boasted Freddie.

"I wasn't either—except when it began to get dark," said his sister. "Then we went in Miss Borden's room, but we couldn't get out there and we couldn't open a window, so I thought of ringing the bell."

"It's a good thing you did," remarked the principal. "Well, everything is all right now. You had better take your sister home, Freddie."

"I'll go with them. It is getting dark fast," said Miss Trent.

"Oh, we're not afraid," said Freddie.

"Well, I'm going your way, anyhow," his teacher answered with a smile. "Come along."

"I'll telephone your mother, Freddie, that you are on the way," offered the principal. "Otherwise she might be worried."

"This is the first time anybody has been

locked in the school in quite a while," remarked the janitor as they all came out. He unlocked the big front doors and Miss Trent and the small Bobbsey twins stepped forth into the dark, for it was now night.

"I supposed you two would go home after I went to the office," explained the teacher. "I never dreamed you would stay to be locked in. It's too bad!"

"Oh, it was fun!" chuckled Freddie. "I only hope nobody found out our secret."

"What secret is that?" asked Miss Trent.

"It's one we have down in our cellar at home," replied Flossie. "I can tell you about it after a while," she said, thinking perhaps it wasn't very polite to have a secret from one's teacher.

"Oh, that's all right, Flossie," said Miss Trent with a smile. "I don't want to know until it's time."

"Nobody knows but us and Dinah," said Freddie. "But after Christmas anybody can see the secret that wants to."

"Yes, after Christmas," agreed Flossie. "Oh, I hope nobody found it out when we were cleaning the boards," she sighed.

"Oh, I hope not!" murmured Miss Trent.

"I don't guess they did," said Freddie hopefully.

Mrs. Bobbsey was just beginning to feel a little worried about the absence of Flossie and Freddie when the principal telephoned and, a little later, brought them home. Bert and Nan had gone down town after class and had not seen the small twins, so their mother did not know what had become of them until she received the telephone message.

"They helped me a lot," said Miss Trent to Mrs. Bobbsey as she went on her way. "But I'm so sorry they got locked in."

"It didn't hurt us," chuckled Freddie. Later, he whispered to Dinah: "Did anybody find out our secret down cellar?"

"No, honey lamb!" answered the fat, black cook. "I kep' good watch. Nobody went nigh de place."

"That's good!" said Flossie.

When Flossie and Freddie awakened next morning they had a grand surprise. Freddie discovered it first. Jumping out of bed he ran to the window to look at the weather. What he saw made him joyfully shout:

"Oh, Flossie! It's snowing! It's snowing! Come and see!"

Flossie's bare feet pattered over the floor of her room. She almost banged her nose against the window in her eagerness. When she saw the white flakes sifting down she shouted:

"Oh! Oh! Oh! Now we can go coasting! Oh, what fun we'll have!"

"Say, it really is snowing!" said Bert as he glanced out after hearing the calls of the younger twins. "Looks like a real storm, Nan!"

"I hope it lasts!" Nan said, and she peered from the window before starting to dress.

It was still snowing when the twins went to school, and the storm kept up even when they had come home.

"Now for some fun!" shouted Bert as he ran to get his sled.

"We'll have a race!" yelled Freddie as he and Flossie got out their sleds, the runners of which had been polished.

The winter fun had started and soon a jolly crowd of children were on their way to the coasting hill.

CHAPTER XI

THROUGH THE ICE

"Hurry, Flossie!" called Freddie Bobbsey to his twin sister as they followed Bert and Nan to the coasting hill. "Hurry up!"

"Please don't go so fast!" she begged. "My sled is heavy to pull."

"I'll help you," kindly offered Freddie. He took hold of the rope of Flossie's coaster, as well as of his own, and then the small twins could go along faster.

"This is great, isn't it?" called Bert to Nan as they ran on through the sifting flakes, their feet making big marks in the snow that already covered the ground.

"It's fine to have snow before Christmas," Nan said. "I always think Christmas is nicer when there's snow."

"Sure! It makes it better for coasting," said Bert. "But it will spoil the skating until we fellows clear off the pond."

There was a small pond not far from the coasting hill, where the Bobbsey twins and their friends had some of their winter fun. This pond had frozen over shortly before the snow storm, and there had been a little skating. But now, with the ice covered by a thick, white blanket, skates were of no use. But it was just the time for sleds.

"Hello, Bert!" called Charlie Mason as he joined the party going to the hill. "Want to have a race?"

"Sure!" Bert answered. "But we'll have to wear the hill down a bit first. We can't race until the hill is smooth."

"It won't take long to make it smooth with all this crowd," declared Charlie. "Here comes Danny Rugg!"

"Yes, and John Marsh," added Bert. "I wish we had a bobsled."

"We'll make one if this snow keeps up," proposed Charlie.

Nan saw Grace Lavine and Nellie Parks and called to them, and soon the three girls ran along by themselves, while Bert and his boy friends, reaching the hill, began to tramp down the snow to pack it well, which would make it better for coasting.

"We'll have a race!" decided Bert as he saw a number of his chums. "It's getting good and smooth now."

"Sure, we'll have a race!" agreed Charlie.

"Oh, if you boys are going to race and go fast we girls can't have any fun!" objected Nan. "Can't you just coast without racing?"

"It's more fun to race," Bert said. "But we'll keep over on one side of the hill and you girls and Flossie and Freddie and the smaller ones can have the other side."

"Yes, I guess that will be all right," Nan decided.

Already several of the children had coasted a little way down the hill, but they could not go very far nor very fast because the snow was not yet well packed and hard.

But the eager feet were fast tramping the snow firm and each time a sled went down the slope it helped to pack the white flakes, making the way harder and smoother.

Flossie and Freddie did their share in helping to get the hill in good condition for coasting. At last Bert and some of the other boys decided that it was all right for a speed contest.

"Now we'll have the race!" called Bert. "But, fellows, keep over on this side so we won't bump into the girls."

"All right," agreed Charlie Mason. "The hill is good and wide."

"I want to race, too, Bert!" called Freddie, as he saw his brother and the older boys lining their sleds on the slope of the hill.

"No, you're too little," Bert objected.

"I am not!" replied Freddie.

"Well, your sled can't go as fast as ours," went on Bert. "You would only be left behind."

"My sled can go faster than yours!" boasted Freddie. "You'll see! I'm going in this race!"

"No, Freddie, you mustn't," said Nan. "Stay over on this side of the hill with Flossie and me. You might get hurt."

"Well, I'm going to race my sled on this side and they can race theirs on that side," Freddie answered. "I'll beat 'em all!"

Bert and his chums paid no attention to Freddie as they got on their sleds in a line to start down the hill. But Freddie did as he saw the older boys doing, lining his sled even with theirs, though keeping on the side of the hill a ways from them.

"All ready?" asked Bert, who had charge of the race.

"All ready!" answered Charlie, Danny and the other boys.

"I'm ready, too!" sang out Freddie.

"No, you mustn't!" cautioned Nan.

"Go!" yelled Bert, giving himself and his sled a push.

The other boys did the same and down the smooth, white slope they started. The race had begun.

"Here I go!" shouted Freddie, and he gave himself a push as Bert had done.

"Oh, Freddie! I wish you wouldn't do that!" sighed Nan.

"He's safe enough if he stays on this side of the hill," said Grace Lavine. "The others won't bump into him."

"I hope not," Nan murmured.

"I'm going to race, too!" suddenly decided Flossie as she got on her sled. She always wanted to do what Freddie did.

"Be careful!" warned Nan, though she knew her little sister would not get anywhere near the big boys, for they were already some distance down the hill.

She need not have worried about Flossie. For that little girl, after coasting a short distance, somehow or other steered her sled the wrong way and it ran into a bank of snow at the side of the hill and came to a stop. Flossie was disappointed but not hurt. With a laugh she jumped off, pulled her sled to the top of the hill and started over again. Many of her little girl chums were doing the same. Nan coasted with the older girls.

Meanwhile the race among Bert and the older boys was going on nicely. They were gliding swiftly down the hill. And, somewhat to Bert's surprise, across the slope, on the side where the girls and small children kept by themselves, Bert saw Freddie coasting along almost even with him.

"Hey, look at your brother, Bert!" shouted Charlie Mason.

"I told him to keep out of this," said Bert.

"Well, he isn't exactly in it," said Danny. "But he's going along as fast as we are."

This was true enough. Though on the far side of the hill, Freddie and his sled were slipping along at a good rate of speed. Freddie was quite proud of himself. Even if the big boys wouldn't let him race with them he could keep up with their sleds.

Bert was now ahead of all the others on his side of the hill. Then a queer thing happened. Freddie's sled shot ahead of all the others, even Bert's, and got to the bottom of the hill first.

"See him go!" cried Charlie.

"His sled is a whizzer!" cried Sam Todd.

"He beat us all!" added John Marsh.

"That's what he did," Bert had to admit. Though Bert's sled was ahead of all those on which his chums sat, still Freddie's sled got to the bottom of the hill before Bert's. So Freddie won the race, though he wasn't really supposed to be in it.

"What kind of sled have you there, Freddie?" asked John Marsh with a laugh, as the crowd of boys began walking up the hill again.

"Oh, it's just a sled I got last year," Freddie answered, not a little proudly. "But guess the reason it went so fast was 'cause I sandpapered the runners."

"I guess that's what did the trick," agreed Bert. "Look, fellows, our runners were all rusty," and he pointed to several yellow streaks in the snow where the rust had rubbed off the sleds that had been taken out of storage for the first coast that day.

"After this, when I race, I'm going to polish my runners," John Marsh said.

"So am I!" echoed the others.

"That was a good race, Freddie," Bert said as they neared the top of the hill. "I'm glad you beat."

"So am I!"

Then the fun went on, while the white flakes whirled merrily down. The boys and girls shouted in glee. For, not only were they having fun, but Christmas was coming.

"Now for a real race!" cried Bert to his boy friends when it was getting dark and almost time to leave the hill. "This will be the last coast, so we'll see who beats. We can have the hill to ourselves," he added. For nearly all the girls and the smaller children had left. Nan had started to go home with Flossie and Freddie, but when Bert spoke about having a last race the small twins begged to be allowed to watch it, so Nan stayed with them.

The snow was now well packed on the hill, and was firm and smooth. The sled runners, too, were now brightly polished and slipped along easily.

"This will be a real race!" called Bert.

With John, Charlie, Danny and several other boys, Bert lined up his sled.

"Go!" he shouted and pushed off.

Down the hill they rushed, faster and faster. Bert's sled was in the lead, and it looked as if he would win the race. Near the bottom of the hill there was a field, off to one side, and in this field was a pond, covered with ice. On top of the ice was a layer of snow.

Just how it happened Bert Bobbsey did not know. But, all of a sudden, his sled swerved to one side, left the hill, and shot over into the field. It slid across the pond. A moment later there was a cracking of broken ice and Bert and his sled plunged into the water.

"Oh! Oh!" cried Nan when she saw what had happened. "There goes Bert through the ice!"

CHAPTER XII

THE SNOWBALL FIGHT

"WHERE'S a rope?"

"Pull him out!"

"Get a fence board or something!"

Bert Bobbsey's chums, forgetting all about the race as soon as they saw what had happened, were shouting as they rolled off their sleds and ran to the pond where Bert had broken through the ice.

Nan and Flossie and Freddie, who had been watching at the top of the hill, ran down the slope toward their brother.

"Oh, will he be drowned?" gasped Flossie.

"I hope not!" murmured Nan.

"That pond isn't very deep," Freddie said. "I know, 'cause I went wading in it last summer to catch frogs. It's hardly up to my knees."

"That's good!" said Nan.

By this time all of Bert's chums who had

been racing with him had jumped off their sleds and reached the edge of the snow-covered icy pond. Bert's sled had coasted almost to the middle before he broke through the ice. But, as Freddie had remembered, the water beneath was not very deep, and Bert was soon able to get to his feet and wade toward the shore. On the way he kept breaking through the ice, his feet making queer, crunching sounds.

"Oh, Bert, are you drowned?" wailed Flossie as she, with Nan and Freddie, reached the edge.

"No, of course I'm not drowned!" he answered with a laugh.

"But I guess you're cold, aren't you?" said Freddie.

"Ye-ye-yes, it is pret-pretty c-c-cold!" Bert answered, and his voice trembled, for he was now shivering.

"You run home as fast as you can!" ordered Charlie Mason. "That will warm you up so you won't catch cold. Come on, I'll run along with you. You bring my sled, Danny."

"Sure I will, and I'll bring Bert's, too. You run along home, Bert."

"Ye-ye-yes, I—I guess that wo-wo-would be a g-g-good thing!" stammered Bert, his teeth chattering, for he was wet, having plunged into the pond at full length. Though the water was only up to his knees when he was standing upright, when he was stretched out on his sled it had come over his back.

"It's queer how this ice broke," said Joe Norton when Bert, accompanied by Charlie, had started for home on a run. "The skating pond held us all right."

"I guess this water is warmer and didn't freeze as thick," said Danny Rugg. "Anyhow, poor Bert plopped in."

"But he wasn't drowned," said Flossie. She seemed to take heart over this.

The accident, though it was not a bad one, brought the day's fun to an end. Those who had remained to watch the last race now began leaving the hill, for it was fast getting dark. Nan, with the small twins, followed more slowly after the crowd of boys who straggled along when Bert had hurried off with Charlie.

Mrs. Bobbsey was surprised and not a little

alarmed when Bert came dashing into the house, dripping wet, and with Charlie helping him along.

"Oh!" she exclaimed. "Was there an accident?"

"Not much of one, Mother," Bert said. "I broke through the ice on the little pond. I'm not hurt, but I'm wet."

"Mah good lan'! Yo' suah am wet!" cried Dinah! "Git yo' things right off, Bert. I'll make some hot lemonade!"

"And I'll get the hot water bag," said his mother.

In a short time Bert, warm and dry, was sipping hot lemonade in bed. Nan and the smaller twins came in a little later and then the story was told.

"And I won the first race!" Freddie insisted on telling, after his father had come home from his lumber office.

"That's what he did," Bert admitted. "I didn't know his sled could go so fast."

"That's 'cause I sandpapered the runners," Freddie said.

In the morning Bert said he felt fine. As it was Saturday he did not have to go to school.

It was hard to be made to stay in the house when there was such jolly fun out of doors, but Mrs. Bobbsey would not let Bert go out, though Nan, Flossie, and Freddie went to the coasting hill. She was afraid Bert was not as well as he thought he was after such a wintry plunge.

"Oh, dear!" sighed Bert. It certainly was hard to stay in on a Saturday when the coasting was so good.

"Maybe," Nan whispered to her brother as she left him in his room to take out Flossie and Freddie, "you could work on your part of our secret while you're here by yourself."

"No, I wouldn't dare," answered Bert, with a shake of his head. "Mother might hear me and then she'd guess."

"That's so, she might," Nan agreed. "Well, we have time enough."

Bert was all right when Monday came and was able to go to school. The storm had stopped but much snow had fallen, more than in many years so early in the season, with Christmas still several weeks off. It looked like a long, cold winter, but this made the children all the happier.

Coming out of school Monday afternoon, Bert caught up a bunch of snow and began making it into a ball.

"Who are you going to throw at?" asked Freddie.

"Nobody," Bert answered. "I just wanted to see if it would pack. It does. It's just right," and Bert made another ball to be sure.

"Are you going to make a snow man?" asked Flossie.

Instead of answering his little sister, Bert called to Charlie Mason across the street.

"Hey, Charlie! It's just right. We'll start and make the fort right away."

"Fine!" answered Charlie. "I'll be right over."

"Oh, are you going to make a snow fort?" asked Freddie, his blue eyes shining with eagerness.

"Yes," replied Bert. "The snow is just right for packing now. We'll make a fort and have a snowball fight."

"Oh, what fun!" cried Freddie. "I'll help!"

"No, you can't play snowball fight with the big boys," objected Nan. "You must come along home with me, Freddie."

"Oh, let me go with Bert!" he pleaded, begging so hard that at last Bert said:

"Well, he can come and help make the fort. We'll need a lot of help for that. But I can't let you be in the snowball fight, Freddie. You might get hurt."

"Couldn't I stay inside the fort and make snowballs for you to throw?" Freddie asked, wistfully.

"Well, I'll see," was all Bert would promise.

Nan took Flossie and went with some of her girl chums to coast on the hill. Freddie, Bert, and many other boys began to make the snow fort. First they rolled big balls of snow and then they put them in line, making a square with one side open. The spaces between the big balls were filled in with snow and after a while the fort was finished.

The boys divided into two groups. One party was to be inside the fort and was to defend it. Bert was captain of this party. The other side, or crowd of boys, was outside the fort and was led by Charlie Mason. They hoped to throw so many snowballs as to drive the defenders out of the fort so they could capture it. Freddie was kept busy making snowballs inside the fort.

"All right. That's enough," said Bert after a while, coming to his small brother. "You run along home now, Freddie. The fight is going to start."

"Can't I stay and see it, Bert?"

"No, you must go home. You might get hurt."

"Oh, Bert! I'll be careful!" Freddie pleaded.

"No, you must go home. Get ready now, fellows!" called Bert to his fort "soldiers" inside the white walls. "Here they come!"

The storming party, or attackers, who pretended they were Indians, began rushing toward the snow fort inside of which Bert and his chums were playing they were early Colonial settlers.

"Wa! Hoo! Woo! Wah!" yelled the "Indians."

"Beat 'em off! Soak 'em! Fire!" cried Bert.

The snowball fight had started.

Bert did not see the figure of Freddie crouching down beside a pile of ammunition in one corner of the fort.

CHAPTER XIII

CHRISTMAS SHOPPING

BANG! Slam! Whack!

Across the top of the white walls of the snow fort came whizzing the "bullets" from the attacking "Indians." Of course the bullets were only soft snowballs that the boys threw. Hard balls were ruled out. Bert and his chums did not want to get any black eyes themselves, neither did they want to blacken the eyes nor bruise the noses of their friendly enemies.

"Soft balls, only, fellows!" Bert had ordered at the start of the fight, and though some of the rougher lads would have liked to make hard, icy balls, this was not allowed.

"Drive 'em back, fellows! Drive 'em back!" yelled Bert as he threw ball after ball over the top of the fort, behind the walls of which he stood with his army of settlers.

"Storm the fort! Drive 'em out!" yelled Charlie Mason, leading his band of "Indians" up as close as he dared to go to the walls of the fort. "Capture 'em!"

At times Charlie and his friends would get quite close; so near, in fact, that it seemed as if they might rush over the walls of snow to drive out the defenders. But at such times Bert and his chums would throw so many volleys of balls that, catching the attacking "Indians" in their faces and on their heads, they would drive them back to the shelter of some trees and bushes where the "Indians" had their camp.

There they would rest and make more balls while talking over the best way to make the next attack. Meanwhile, Bert and his friends would pile up more balls to use as ammunition when the next attack came.

"Why can't we go around to the back and get in the fort that way?" asked Dick Hatton, who was one of the "Indians." There was no wall at the back and it would seem easy to get in that way.

"No, that isn't fair," replied Charlie. "Bert didn't want to take time to make a fort with four sides, so we made one with only three and we made a rule that there was to be fighting on the three sides. The fourth side is out of bounds."

"Oh, all right," agreed Dick. "I wondered why we couldn't go in that way."

"Come on now!" called Charlie after a while. "We'll try again. Rush 'em hard, fellows! Take plenty of balls and let's drive 'em out."

"Sure! We'll drive 'em out!" yelled his chums.

Inside the fort Bert and his boys saw the attack coming again. Bert looked to the pile of snowballs. There were not many left and he and his army had used up most of the loose snow inside the three walls of the fort. To get more ammunition they would have to go outside.

"I wish I'd let Freddie stay and make some more balls," thought Bert as he saw the next attack coming. "But I guess he went home."

He did not yet see a small figure crouched behind a pile of snow.

"Drive 'em back! Drive 'em back!" yelled Bert as the "Indians" neared the fort, yelling and throwing balls. "Don't let 'em capture us! Drive 'em back!"

At the same time Charlie and his crowd shouted:

"Drive 'em out! Drive 'em out!"

The air was filled with flying snowballs. But, though Bert and his chums sent dozens of them on the heads and into the faces of the "Indians," the attacking party still came bravely on.

"More balls! More balls!" yelled Bert to some boys back of him and a crowd who stood close to the inside walls of the fort. This second line of boys was supposed to make the ammunition, or snowballs, and pass it to the first fighting line.

"We can't give you any more balls," said Harry Smith.

"Why not?" cried Bert.

"Because all the snow in the fort is used up," Harry answered. "If we make more balls we'll have to go outside."

"Got to have more balls!" yelled Bert. "Look at 'em coming at us!"

The attackers, well supplied with ammunition, were swarming toward the fort. Unless the defenders could drive them back the place would be captured.

"More balls! More balls!" begged Bert.

"No more balls!" answered Harry, who was the leader of the crowd making the white "bullets."

"Then we've lost the fort!" said Bert.

But suddenly a shrill, little voice cried:

"Here, Bert! Here are a lot of balls I made!"

Out from behind a pile of snow just inside the fort, where he had hidden after Bert told him to go home, jumped Freddie Bobbsey. The little fellow's arms were filled with round, white balls. Behind him was a pile of the snow "bullets."

"Here you are!" cried Freddie.

"Good for you!" shouted Bert. "Get those balls, fellows, and drive 'em back!"

With the new supply of ammunition, thus unexpectedly provided, the tide of the fight turned. Unable to stand the rain of snowballs thrown at them, Charlie's crowd turned about and ran away.

"After 'em! After 'em!" shouted Bert. "If we drive 'em past the trees we win!"

Out of the fort leaped Bert's "settlers," now with a good supply of ammunition, while that of the "Indians" ran low. Past the trees Charlie and his boys were chased under a rain of the snowball bullets until they had all scattered and the defenders of the fort had that place all to themselves and the space in front no longer held any enemy. Freddie ran along with Bert, throwing snowballs at the retreating band of "Indians."

"We win! We win!" cried Bert's friends.

"Fight's over!" said Bert, for it was now getting dusk.

"It would have been over for us before this if your little brother hadn't made those balls," said Tom Johnson.

"That's right," Bert agreed. "Why didn't you go home when I told you to, Freddie?"

"Oh, 'cause," was all Freddie said.

The other boys laughed.

So the first snowball fight ended, and Freddie Bobbsey was the hero of it, though he did not quite understand how it had come about. When Bert told him to run home Freddie hid himself in the fort and made a lot of extra snowballs which turned the fight in his brother's favor.

There was great fun in the Bobbsey home

that night when the story of the snow fight and Freddie's part in it was told.

"But you might have got a bang in the eye," said Flossie.

"I might," chuckled Freddie, "but I didn't."

The next Saturday Mrs. Bobbsey said to the children:

"Do you want to come Christmas shopping with me?"

"Oh, yes!" cried Nan, Bert, Flossie and Freddie.

"All right, get ready," said their mother. "We must go down town and see what Santa Claus has for Grandpa and Grandma and for your uncles and aunts, my dears." For the Bobbsey twins, knowing that Santa Claus had much to do, always helped their mother pick out presents for their many relatives.

In a little while they were ready and got into the car which Mrs. Bobbsey was to drive down town. The weather was clear and cold, and there had been no more storms since the one big one just before the fight at the fort.

Just as Mrs. Bobbsey was about to go, Freddie cried:

"Oh, wait a minute!" He started to get out of the auto.

"What's the idea?" asked Bert.

"I—I forgot something," said Freddie with a look at Flossie. "I—I have to go down cellar!" and back to the house he ran.

CHAPTER XIV

FLOSSIE'S CAKE

"WHERE are you going, Freddie?" his mother asked. She was ready to start the auto and did not like being thus delayed.

"I'll be right back—in a minute!" he called over his shoulder.

"Well, of all things!" exclaimed Nan. "Just when we get ready to do our Christmas shopping Freddie has to go back for a handkerchief or something!"

"I don't b'lieve he has gone back to get a handkerchief," said Flossie in rather a timid voice.

"Well, what did he go back for?" asked Bert.

"I—I guess he wanted to—to go down cellar," said the little girl.

"What for?" demanded Nan. "What's down cellar, anyhow, but a lot of cobwebs?"

"There must be something more than cobwebs in our cellar," observed Bert. "Flossie and Freddie have been going up and down there a lot lately."

"Have you, Flossie?" asked Mrs. Bobbsey. She had been so busy with the approach of Christmas that she had not given much heed to what the children were doing as long as they kept out of mischief.

"Oh, yes," Flossie answered. "Freddie and I go down cellar sometimes. But it doesn't hurt anybody."

"You'll get hurt if you slip and fall," said Bert. "Hey, come on, Freddie!" he called. "You're holding up the game."

"Go and see what he is doing, Bert," Nan urged.

"No! Don't! I'll go and get Freddie!" Flossie quickly offered.

"Yes, and then you'll go down cellar and you and Freddie will talk about that big secret of yours!" chuckled Bert. "Then we'll be later than ever. You stay here, Flossie. I'll go and see what's keeping Freddie and make him come."

"Oh, no! No!" cried the little girl, and she seemed so worried that Mrs. Bobbsey said:

"The children have a right to their little secret, Bert, just as much as you and Nan have."

"Oh, have we a secret?" asked Nan with a laugh and a quick look at Bert, which showed her surprise.

"Well," went on Mrs. Bobbsey with a smile, "I have seen you and Bert going into the garage many times lately. I rather guessed that you might have a secret there as Flossie and Freddie seemingly have down in the cellar. But I'm not going to try to find out what either secret is," she ended, and Nan and Bert looked much relieved.

"I guess Freddie will come back in a minute," said Flossie and she, too, breathed easier, now that it was certain no one would be allowed to follow her small brother to the dark basement. "Here he comes now," she went on, as Freddie appeared around the corner of the house, running along the snow-bordered path. Sam Johnson had shoveled all the paths after the snowfall.

"Here I am," announced Freddie as he got into the auto again.

"Just as if we couldn't see that!" said Nan with a smile as she made room for him.

"I had to go down to shut a window," went on Freddie.

"What difference did it make if a cellar window was open?" asked Bert. He winked one eye at Nan.

"Don't tease them," said Mrs. Bobbsey in a low voice.

"I had to shut the window," went on Freddie, and then he whispered to Flossie: "I thought maybe it might snow while we were down town doing the Christmas shopping."

"Yes, it is best to keep the cellar windows closed in winter," said Mrs. Bobbsey with a smile. "And now, if you are all ready, we'll start off once more," she said.

"Oh, yes, I'm all ready," announced Freddie.

"So'm I," echoed his twin sister. So they started.

Mrs. Bobbsey parked the car in a garage near the shopping center of Lakeport and then she and the children began to visit various shops and toy stores. There were many relatives to whom Mr. and Mrs. Bobbsey sent

Christmas presents, and the children also sent little gifts to friends, neighbors, and relatives. There were many things to be bought in different stores, and, to their delight, Flossie and Freddie, for the first time, were allowed to pick some of the gifts themselves—gifts that were to be sent to cousins in distant towns and cities.

Bert had wandered to the book counter where he was looking over some of the new holiday volumes, and Nan, with her mother, was looking at some bureau toilet sets of combs, brushes, and hand mirrors, when Flossie and Freddie wandered, as you may guess, to the toy counter.

The eyes of Flossie gazed at a wonderful, big doll, which looked so much like a real baby that several women stopped to admire it. Freddie had caught sight of a new kind of "squirting fire engine," as he called it. He had one, but he was always looking at new ones. Then Flossie reached out a hand and gently touched the wonderful doll. At once a voice exclaimed:

"Oh, hello! Please to meet you! Won't you come in?"

Flossie was so surprised that she jumped back, withdrawing her hand so quickly that she knocked another doll off the counter. But she caught it in time to prevent its being broken.

"Oh, did you hear that?" murmured Flossie. "That doll talked to me!"

By this time the young woman waiting on that counter came up and smiled at the children as Freddie, who had also rushed up, took the doll Flossie had knocked off and put it back on the counter. The clerk said:

"That is the very latest doll. She has a phonograph inside her and she talks."

"Oh, how wonderful!" murmured Flossie. "Did I make her talk?"

"If you touched her hand you did," the clerk said. "She is wound up, and to make the voice sound you have only to touch the right hand, like this."

She gently touched the doll as Flossie had done, and once more the phonograph voice came out of the make-believe child.

"I wish I would get a doll like that for Christmas," sighed Flossie.

"I'd rather have that big hook and ladder

truck," said Freddie, pointing at one next to the "squirter," as he called the engine. "My own engine is better than that one, but I'd like a hook and ladder truck."

"How would you like some ice cream?" asked a voice back of the little twins. Turning in surprise they saw their mother and Bert and Nan.

"Ice cream?" exclaimed Flossie in surprise.

"I'd love it!" cried Freddie.

"Then come and we shall get some," his mother went on. "We have about finished our Christmas shopping and it is quite warm in this store. Did you see anything you liked, my dears?" she asked the small twins.

"Oh, Mother!" Flossie ejaculated. "The most wonderful doll! She talked when I touched her hand!"

"And look at this swell hook and ladder truck!" cried Freddie.

Mrs. Bobbsey admired these toys and then led the children to the soda counter of the store where they had some refreshment. Later they visited a few other shops, but none so wonderful, Flossie and Freddie thought, as the one where they had seen the talking doll and the big, red hook and ladder truck.

"Well," remarked Mrs. Bobbsey when they reached home late that afternoon, "I think most of my Christmas shopping is done. The rest," she said with a smile, "I am going to leave to Santa Claus."

For the children the best season of all the year was drawing near. It would soon be Christmas. School would close shortly before the holiday and remain closed until after New Year's Day.

"And what fun we'll have!" cried Nan, dancing about. "I am going to have a party for some of the girls."

"I'm going to get the fellows to build a bigger snow fort and we'll have a grand snowball battle," decided Bert.

"If I get a new doll for Christmas," said Flossie in a low voice, "I'll have a party for her and invite all my old dolls."

"I'm going to sandpaper the runners of my sled some more," was what Freddie said. "Then I can beat anybody on the hill."

"I hope you do," laughed Bert. "And I hope I don't crack through any more ice."

"If you are going to have a party for your girl friends, Nan," said Mrs. Bobbsey, "I think it would be nice if you baked them a special cake all by yourself. Dinah will show you how to do it."

"Oh, that's great, Mother!" cried Nan. "I'm going to ask Dinah now. How wonderful!"

"I'll come and help you," offered Flossie, while Bert went off by himself to read and Freddie got out his "squirter" engine to make sure it worked, though he was not allowed to put any real water in the tank while playing with the machine in the house.

Nan knew something about cooking and once had made a cake and a batch of biscuits. For once upon a time she and her brothers and sister had to keep house all by themselves, as told in the book of that name. Mr. and Mrs. Bobbsey went away and Aunt Sallie Pry, who was engaged to look after things, was taken ill, so most of the work fell on Nan.

"But I've never made a Christmas cake, Dinah," said Nan as she and Flossie went out to the kitchen.

"I'll show you," offered the kind, black cook.

Flossie watched with eager eyes as Dinah showed Nan how to mix up the cake dough, put it into greased pans, and then slip the pans into the oven. It was a sort of sample cake that Dinah and Nan made that afternoon, and they were so busy they did not pay much heed to what Flossie did. But after the several layers of the sample cake had been taken out of the oven and Nan was putting chocolate on them, Flossie spied the mixing bowl which had some dough left in it and asked:

"May I have this?"

"Oh, yes, I reckon so, honey lamb," answered Dinah, not looking to see what it was, so intent was she on showing Nan how properly to apply the chocolate to the cake.

Flossie busied herself with quite a bit of dough that she scraped out of the bowl.

"I'll surprise 'em," she murmured.

At last Nan's cake was finished and she insisted on Dinah's coming with her to show it to Mrs. Bobbsey.

"For you helped me, Dinah," said Nan.

"Well, yo' kin bake the nex' cake **by** yo'se'f," said the cook with a smile.

When Dinah and Nan left the kitchen Flossie had the place to herself and she was very busy for a few moments. Then she went in to see how her mother liked Nan's cake.

"It is very nice, indeed," said Mrs. Bobsey, admiring it. "I hope your Christmas cake turns out as well."

"I hope so," murmured Nan.

Dinah began to sniff the air. So did Mrs. Bobbsey. So did Nan. They all sniffed, and Dinah cried:

"Suffin's burnin'!"

"Oh, I guess it's my cake!" cried Flossie, making a dash for the kitchen whence came a most decided smell of something on fire.

CHAPTER XV

Flossie Bobbsey had what Freddie would have called a "head start" on the others in the race for the kitchen. But Nan, her mother, and Dinah were not far behind. Nan was holding the cake she had just baked, and, for fear of dropping this, she could not go very fast. So her mother got ahead of her. Fat Dinah was last, of course. She never could go very fast.

Flossie reached the kitchen first and she gave a wail of dismay as she saw a cloud of bluish smoke around the stove.

"Oh, my lovely cake!" she sighed.

"What cake?" asked her mother. "I didn't know you were baking a cake."

"It's all burned!" and Flossie was almost crying now.

"Well, whatever it is, I should say it was burning," remarked Mrs. Bobbsey. She got

147

a holder-cloth and opened the oven door. A cloud of smoke rolled out.

"Is there—is there anything left of my nice cake?" faltered the little girl.

"I'm afraid not," Mrs. Bobbsey answered. "Hand me the poker, Dinah, please," she went on as Nan, followed by the fat cook, reached the kitchen.

"Oh, am mah honey lamb burned?" asked Dinah, not able to see Flossie very clearly on account of the smoke.

"No, I'm all right, Dinah," the little girl answered. "But my lovely cake is all spoiled."

"Yes, I should say it was quite spoiled," agreed Mrs. Bobbsey as, with the poker, she pulled the pan from the oven. In the middle of the pan was a smoldering lump as black as a coal.

"That's my—my cake!" and poor Flossie was now crying in real earnest.

"Oh, I'm so sorry!" murmured Nan. "You may have some of this cake I just made, Flossie."

"How did she come to be baking a cake?" asked Mrs. Bobbsey as she set the smoldering pan on the back steps while Dinah opened a window to let out the smoke that filled the kitchen.

"I guess Flossie took some of the cake dough I had left over from my cake," explained Nan, "and she put that in the oven. But there was only a little bit."

"There—there was enough for a cake for my dolls and me!" sighed Flossie. "I put the dough on a pan just as Dinah did. What made it burn?"

"The oven was too hot, my dear, you spread the dough out too thin, and you didn't watch your cake. You must always watch your cake when it is baking, to make sure it doesn't burn," said her mother.

"I must remember that when I make my Christmas cake," said Nan.

When the piece of cinder, that had once been a cake, had cooled out in the back porch, Flossie looked at it. Then her mother again told her that she had spread the dab of dough out so thin on the pan that, in an extra hot oven, it had soon cooked through and had started to burn.

"Next time I'll put in more dough if Dinah will give it to me," said Flossie.

"I'll gib yo' a lot, honey lamb," murmured Dinah. "I didn't s'pose yo' was really wantin' to make a cake when yo' ast me fo' whut dough was left over from Nan's. Nex' time yo' have better luck, honey lamb!"

"I hope so," sighed Flossie.

After that first snowstorm, following which had been held the great fight at the fort where Freddie had been such a hero, there came a spell of warm weather, and then rain. The rain washed away most of the snow and the Bobbsey twins felt sad.

"I hoped we'd have snow for Christmas," said Nan.

"Oh, there is time enough for more snow before the holidays," her mother said.

"Anyhow, the rain will make the skating good on the pond if we get a freeze," decided Bert. "We can have fun skating if we can't have any making forts and going coasting."

It rained so hard one day that Mrs. Bobbsey decided the children should stay home from school. When they heard this Nan and Bert looked quickly at each other and Bert said:

"We can finish now, I guess."

"Yes," Nan agreed.

A little later, under a big umbrella, Nan and Bert made a dash for the garage.

"What are they going out there for?" asked Flossie.

"I don't know, my dear," answered Mrs. Bobbsey.

"I s'pose it's that secret," whispered Flossie to herself. "Well, anyhow, I don't care. Freddie and I have a secret of our own!"

As Nan had, in a way, deserted her, Flossie had to make up some amusement of her own, and this she did with some of her dolls up in the attic.

As for Freddie, he got out his fire engine that squirted real water. Seeing so much rain coming down outside made the little boy want to have some real fun with his toy.

"If I take it down cellar could I squirt it?" he asked his mother.

"Oh, yes, I guess so," she answered. "But don't get yourself wet and dirty."

"I won't," promised Freddie. "Where's Flossie?" he asked as he got his fire engine from his box of toys under the stairs.

"She's up in the attic having a play party for her dolls," replied Mrs. Bobbsey.

"Where are Nan and Bert?"

"They went out in the garage."

"Oh," murmured Freddie, and then he asked no more questions for a time. Down in the cellar he had good fun playing with his fire engine. He made it pump water over in the coal bin, as he thought that would not do any harm. But there was a certain corner from which Freddie kept well away with his "squirter."

"I don't want to get the secret wet," Freddie murmured.

Though it was fun playing by himself with his fire engine, he knew it would be much jollier if he had Flossie with him. Of course, some of his boy chums would be better, for they could be firemen and Freddie could be the chief. But Flossie was also a good chum to play with.

"But the way it rains now," mused Freddie, "I guess none of the boys will come out. I'll go up and see if Flossie won't come down here and play engine with me."

He went up the steep cellar steps and had

almost reached the top when he heard Nan and Bert entering the kitchen from their visit to the garage. Freddie did not want his older sister and brother to see him coming out of the cellar, for fear they would ask him something about the secret.

"I'll go back down and wait until they get out of the way," he said to himself.

Freddie turned to go down, but his foot slipped on a step and down the cellar stairs he tumbled, bumping himself very hard.

"Oh!" he cried. "Oh! Oh!" Then he held his hand over his mouth to keep back the moans of pain.

CHAPTER XVI

NAN'S DISAPPOINTMENT

FREDDIE BOBBSEY fell all the way to the bottom of the cellar stairs, almost from the top. The cellar bottom was of hard concrete, but at the foot of the stairs Dinah had placed an old mat, so those who came up, after putting coal on the furnace, could wipe their feet and not carry so much dirt into her kitchen.

It was on this soft mat that Freddie ended his tumble and it was a good thing the mat was there or the little boy might have gotten a much harder knock than he did. As it was he received some painful bruises on his arms and legs and a scratch on his head that bled a little.

"But I mustn't cry! I mustn't yell!" thought Freddie as, with his hand over his mouth, he bravely kept back his expressions of pain. "If I yell," he reasoned, "Bert and

Nan will come running down here or Mother may come down and then they'll find out our secret!"

That would never do. Freddie felt that he must do all he could to keep the secret until the time came to tell about it.

For a moment after landing with a thump on the old mat, the little boy remained quiet, not moving or crying out, though he felt it would have helped his pains a lot just to give a few good yells. But he wasn't going to do it.

"I hope I didn't break any of my arms or legs," mused Freddie.

The pain, though severe, was not quite so bad now, and he ventured to move first his arms and then his legs, straightening himself out from the lump into which he had tumbled.

"Well, I guess nothing is broken," Freddie went on as he found he could stretch out and bend back both his arms and legs, though to do this pained him a little. "I'll see if I can get up."

There is one lucky thing about children. When they fall they seem to go down like a rubber ball instead of like a brick, and so they very seldom break any bones. It was so in Freddie's case. He found that he could get up, and he could soon walk about the cellar where he had turned on an electric bulb to see to play with his fire engine.

But it was painful to move, and his head hurt. However, he had kept back his first cries of pain and he made up his mind he would not cry out now to bring Nan or Bert running down to see what was the matter and, possibly, to discover the precious secret.

Freddie's head hurt him so much that he put his hand to the most tender spot and when he looked at his fingers there was blood on them.

"Oh, I must be cut!" he murmured, and this frightened him a little.

However, he took heart when he saw that there was not much blood on his hand. Then, recalling what his mother had once done for Flossie when she fell and cut her head, Freddie went to the stationary tubs and washed his bruised head.

The cold water made him feel much better. His aches and pains in his arms and legs were also growing less, and he thought he had better go up now, for either Nan or Bert might soon miss him and come looking for him.

Having put away his engine, after emptying the water out of the tank, Freddie started up the cellar steps, taking care to make no slips.

"I don't want to fall again," he said.

Nan and Bert were in the kitchen when he entered, but they were so busy getting some bread and jam from Dinah that they did not see Freddie come out through the cellar door. It was not until he stood in the middle of the room that they turned and saw him.

"Hello! Where'd you come from?" asked Bert.

Before Freddie could answer Nan's quick eyes observed the blood on the little boy's forehead and on his hand.

"Oh, what happened?" she cried.

"I—I just sort of bumped my head and scratched it," was the answer.

"Oh, you poor thing!" cried his sister. "Bert, do something!"

"What'll I do?"

"Call Mother! Get a doctor!"

Nan was getting excited.

"I don't need any doctor!" said Freddie, bravely. "It isn't much of a cut. I put cold water on it and that's why it looks like so much blood. I'm all right."

"Let me look at you," ordered Bert. And when he had gently inspected his small brother's head he said to worried Nan:

"It isn't anything—just a scratch. Wait, I'll wash it off a bit more and then you can clean yourself, Freddie."

Though it hurt Freddie when Bert washed the cut again, the little fellow did not cry out nor whimper. And he was glad he had not yelled when falling down the stairs.

"For," he said to Flossie afterward, "if Nan and Bert had come down to pick me up, they sure would have seen the secret."

"Was it out?" asked Flossie in a whisper. "I mean, was our secret out around the cellar where they could see it?"

"Part of it was," Freddie answered.

"Oh, then it's a good thing Bert and Nan didn't go down," agreed the little girl.

When the little boy was going to bed, Mrs. Bobbsey noticed the lump and swelling on Freddie's head and she meant to ask how it happened. She did not connect it with his play in the cellar that rainy afternoon. But just as she was about to question Freddie, Mr. Bobbsey called her to the telephone so she forgot all about it, and Freddie was glad of it.

"For I wouldn't want her to find out the secret, either," he said to Flossie when he bade her goodnight.

"Oh, no! Mother mustn't find out!" Flossie agreed.

The rain stopped, the weather turned cold, and there was good fun skating on the frozen ponds. Flossie and Freddie took their skates and had some good times on the ice. Nan went gliding around with her girl chums, and Bert and his boy friends got up a skating race. Then came more snow.

It was one Friday afternoon when the Bobbsey twins came home from school a bit earlier than usual that, while Flossie and Freddie hurried up to the attic to get something with which to play, Bert said to Nan:

"You can go down town with me now, can't you?"

"Oh, yes," was the answer. "We ought to get finished soon, now."

"I think we shall, after one more trial," said Bert. "So it's important that you come with me now."

"All right," Nan agreed. "I'll come in a little while. Wait out in the back yard for me. I have only to comb my hair and slip on another dress."

Nan had finished arraying herself for the secret trip down town with Bert when the front door bell rang. As Nan knew her Mother was at the telephone and Dinah was in the midst of some kitchen work, she went to the front door herself.

Usually Nan liked company; but when she saw who the visitors were this time she made a wry face—after turning her head—and murmured:

"Oh, bother!"

On the steps stood Mrs. Blander and her daughter Lulu, a girl about Nan's age, but one who was so silly and tiresome that Nan could not bear her.

"I have come to call on your mother, Nan," said Mrs. Blander. "While we are talking you can play with Lulu. How is your mother?"

"She—she's well," faltered Nan, a great disappointment in her heart. "Won't you come in?"

Mrs. Blander and Lulu entered. Nan saw her chances of getting to town with Bert that afternoon slipping away.

"Oh, dear!" she sighed.

CHAPTER XVII

BERT'S QUEER TALK

"Come right in, Lulu, and make yourself at home," invited Mrs. Blander to her freckled daughter. That was Mrs. Blander's way—always making herself at home in the houses of other folks.

"I'm coming, Ma," said Lulu, giggling. "I'm coming in."

"I wish you weren't," Nan thought to herself. But of course she was too polite to say this aloud. An unwelcome guest must not be made to feel unhappy. So Nan ushered the visitors into the living room and, excusing herself, went to call her mother.

"Who is it?" asked Mrs. Bobbsey, preparing to come downstairs.

"Mrs. Blander and Lulu," Nan reported. "Oh, Mother, do I have to stay in?"

"Why, I think so, Nan. Mrs. Blander came to call on me and you must entertain Lulu."

"But, Mother, I don't like Lulu."

"That isn't any excuse when anyone comes to call on you. Go back now and say that I will be there in a moment. Meanwhile, entertain Lulu and her mother as best you can."

"But, Mother," sighed Nan, "Bert and I were going down town this afternoon. It's very important! He is waiting for me and if I have to talk to that tiresome Lulu and entertain her I'll never get away. Mrs. Blander always stays so long!"

"Yes, I know, Nan dear! She does make long visits and I sometimes get tired myself. But we must be polite and not show that we're tired. I'm sorry, but it can't be helped. Run along now and I'll be down in a moment. Your trip with Bert can wait."

"No, Mother, that's just it! We can't wait! It's very important——"

But Mrs. Bobbsey went into her room to give one last touch to her hair and did not pay any more heed to poor Nan's protests. Of course this talk between mother and daughter had taken place where the visitors could not hear.

"I don't care!" murmured Nan as she went

back to the living room. "I think it's mean they had to come just at this time! I promised Bert I'd go with him to the music store and now I can't!"

What was so important about going to the music store down town with her brother Nan did not even whisper. It was too much of a secret for that, and Christmas was not far away.

"Mother will be right down," Nan said as she went back to where Mrs. Blander and Lulu were sitting. "It's nice weather, isn't it?" asked Nan. She felt that this was the right way to start a talk by which she could "entertain" the visitors until Mrs. Bobbsey came.

"Yes, nice for this time of year," admitted Mrs. Blander. "But I don't like so much snow."

"Oh, I think the snow is lovely!" exclaimed Nan. "It doesn't seem like Christmas unless we have snow."

"Snow is entirely useless!" decided Mrs. Blander, with a grim, smirking smile. "It clutters up the streets and brings a lot of dirt into the house."

"Oh, I love snow!" murmured Nan. Really,

these visitors were getting "on her nerves," as she told Grace Lavine afterward. But Nan thought the weather was something safe to talk about.

"I hate snow!" exclaimed Lulu. "I get my feet wet and then I catch cold and have the snuffles."

"Yes, poor Lulu suffers dreadfully from colds," said her mother. "I shall be glad when winter is over."

Poor Lulu suffered from "snuffles" and many freckles. Of course, those things weren't her fault, Nan knew.

"But it is her fault that she's such a pest!" Nan told her chum Grace a few days later in speaking of the visit.

Mrs. Bobbsey came in and greeted her visitors politely, and then Mrs. Blander, motioning to the piano, said:

"Lulu has learned some new music. I'm sure she would like to play for you. Wouldn't you, Lulu?"

"Yes, Ma!"

"Then play your new piece."

Nan almost groaned aloud. She knew something of Lulu's music; the striking of wrong notes, playing out of time, and with about as much expression as if a monkey turned a hand organ. But there was no help for it.

"I am sure we shall be glad to hear Lulu play," murmured Mrs. Bobbsey. She would have been glad if Lulu really could have played. Mrs. Bobbsey was a good musician and Nan could play very well for her age.

Lulu took her place on the piano bench while Nan tried not to look at her mother and make a funny face. But it was hard work. Nan wanted, most dreadfully, to make a funny face to show that she knew what was coming. But Mrs. Bobbsey was talking to Mrs. Blander.

Lulu began to play and it was just as Nan had expected. Lulu hit more wrong notes than right ones, it seemed, and she had very little idea of time. The result was distressing to the nerves of those who knew and loved music.

"I don't know this piece very well," Lulu said in excuse after she had brought it to an end with a crash of discords.

"She got it from her teacher only last week," explained Mrs. Blander with a smirk.

"But I think she plays it very well. You might do it over again, Lulu."

But Nan could not stand this. And she knew her mother's nerves were on edge from the performance. So Nan, making up her mind she would have to go through with being polite to her caller, said:

"Come, Lulu, and I will show you some Christmas presents I have bought for my little cousins in the country."

"Yes, Lulu, run along with Nan," urged Mrs. Blander. "I want to talk to Mrs. Bobbsey. You girls will have a good time together."

This time Nan could not help making a funny face at the mention of "a good time," but she took care to make the face when she was near the door, so no one saw her.

Lulu, with her "snuffles" and her freckles, followed Nan upstairs and the two ladies talked together. It was no pleasure for Nan to show her gifts to the caller, but she went through with it as politely as she could.

Meanwhile Bert was waiting for Nan to join them, for they had planned to go down town that afternoon. Having waited for some time and finding that Nan did not come out, Bert went to the house.

"Hey, Nan!" he called from outside, not wanting to go in as his feet were snowy. "Hey, Nan! Don't be all day!"

"Yo' mustn't call yo' sister," warned Dinah from the kitchen where she was cooking.

"Why not?" asked Bert. "She is going down town with me."

"She can't go now," said Dinah.

"Why not?"

"She's done got comp'ny."

"Company! Who?"

"Mrs. Blander an' Miss Lulu."

"Oh, for cats' sake!" groaned Bert. "Those pests! They'll stay all night! We'll never get down town! Hey, Nan!" he cried desperately. "Are you coming?"

Up in her room, where she was showing Lulu the gifts, Nan heard her brother's call. Raising the window she said:

"I can't come now, Bert."

"Well, when can you come?"

"Oh, I don't know!" answered Nan desperately. "Go on away, Bert."

"What does he want?" asked Lulu.

"Oh, he wants me to go somewhere with him," sighed Nan, wishing with all her heart that she could go.

"Boys are a bother!" exclaimed Lulu. "Aren't they?"

"Brothers like Bert aren't," said Nan, loyally.

"I don't like boys," decided Lulu. She had no brothers, being an only child. "Go on, show me what else you got."

So poor Nan had to keep on "entertaining" her guest while outside Bert shouted:

"I'll come back in a little while. You be ready then. It's getting late!"

What could Nan say in front of Lulu? Nothing. She just had to go on showing the Christmas gifts.

Bert came back in a little while and called again:

"Ho, Nan! If you're coming down town, come on! It'll soon be dark!"

Once more Nan had to answer out of the window:

"I can't come now, Bert."

"Well, when can you come?"

Nan looked at Lulu, who had her back

turned. Nan made a funny face and sadly said:

"I don't know, Bert. I—I guess you'd better not wait for me."

"I'll wait a little while longer," he promised. "Hurry up!"

Poor Nan couldn't hurry. Mrs. Blander and her daughter showed no signs of going. Bert made one last appeal and when he found Nan could not come out and that it was getting dusk, he went to the garage alone.

It was there, a little later, that Flossie and Freddie, coming back from a visit to some friends, heard Bert's voice making strange talk in the building. Bert was uttering loud words as he paced up and down beside the car, and as there was a light in the place, Flossie and Freddie could see that their brother was all alone.

"Something must be done! Something must be done!" proclaimed Bert loudly.

"Who—who's he talking to?" whispered Flossie.

"Nobody," answered Freddie.

"Why, he must be talking to *somebody*," insisted the little blue-eyed girl.

"Well, he isn't," declared Freddie. "You can see for yourself. Bert is in there all alone."

"Oh, so he is!" Flossie murmured. "How queer!"

Bert again loudly declaimed:

"I will not do it! No, not in a thousand years!"

Flossie and Freddie looked strangely at each other on hearing this queer talk. What did it mean? Why was Bert acting in such an odd way, all by himself, in the garage? Had anything happened?

Flossie and Freddie were quite ready to believe this. Especially when a moment later they heard a voice calling to them from the kitchen door.

"Flossie! Freddie! Come here! Hurry!"

CHAPTER XVIII

DISCOVERED

"COME on! Run!" said Freddie.

"Oh, something must have happened!" exclaimed Flossie as she turned away from the garage and hastened with her brother toward the house whence came the voice of Nan, calling.

"Maybe it's about Bert acting so oddly in the garage," went on Freddie.

"Yes! Didn't he talk queerly?" commented Flossie.

When they reached the house in the dusk of the evening, only Nan awaited them in the kitchen doorway. The visitors had gone. Nan was free of Lulu, but had missed the trip to town with Bert. Nan's calling had nothing to do with what Bert did in the garage. When Nan saw the small twins she was not in the least excited, so nothing could have happened —that is, nothing much.

"Where have you two been?" asked Nan of the little twins.

"Over to Harry Ford's," answered Freddie.

"We found some old bells up in our attic," went on Flossie, "and we took some over to Harry."

"He's going to put a bell on his sled and I'm going to put one on my sled," said Freddie.

"And I'm going to have one on mine!" added Flossie. "But why did you call us, Nan? And what's Bert talking to himself for out in the garage?"

"Is he doing that?" asked Nan, with a queer look on her face.

"Yes, we heard him!" said Freddie and Flossie in a sort of duet.

"Well, I called you to help me make some snow cream," went on Nan, not answering the other question. "We need something for dessert and Mrs. Blander and Lulu stayed so late I didn't have time to help Dinah make any. So Mother said I could make snow cream and I want you two to help me get the snow."

"Oh, goodie!" exclaimed Freddie, capering about in glee.

"I'll get a lot of snow," offered Flossie.

This was not the first time the little twins had helped to make this quick and delicious dessert. Snow pudding is something like ice cream. After Nan had beaten up some milk, eggs, sugar, and flavoring in a bowl, she stirred into it some clean snow, so that the mixture was like a soft ice cream. It could be quickly made and Mrs. Bobbsey often let Nan try her skill in this way.

"Snow pudding is lovely dessert," said Flossie as she watched Nan stirring it in the kitchen while Dinah went on getting supper.

"What made Mrs. Blander and Lulu stay so late?" asked Freddie.

"Oh, I don't know," sighed Nan. She had been much disappointed at not being able to go down town with her twin brother.

"Late! I should say they did stay late!" complained Bert, who came in from the garage just then. "I thought they'd never go!"

"So did I," sighed Nan. "And you kept yelling at me to come out."

"Well, you said you were coming."

"I know. But I couldn't. I had to entertain that freckled Lulu."

"Ha! Ha!" laughed Bert. "I'm glad that it

was you instead of me. Did she play the piano for you?"

"She tried to," said Nan. "But I thought she would say something about you yelling at me so much."

"I thought maybe if I yelled enough she would take the hint and go home," said Bert.

"Well, she didn't," retorted Nan. "And you made me so fussy! Why couldn't you go down town by yourself?"

"You know it wouldn't have been any good for me to go alone," said Bert. "We have to go together. And the time is getting short now. We'll have to go in a couple of days or it will be too late."

"I can go next time," Nan promised.

"Go where?" asked Flossie when the snow cream was set outside to keep cold until needed for the table. "What were you and Bert going down town for?"

The older twins exchanged laughing looks and Nan said:

"It's a secret!"

"A big secret!" added Bert.

"Was it a secret when you talked so loud

to yourself out in the garage?" asked Freddie.

"What! Were you hanging around there
spying on me?" asked Bert quickly.

"We just came past and we heard you,"
Freddie said. "What were you talking to
yourself for?"

"Oh, that's a **secret**, too," chuckled Bert,
looking at Nan.

"Tell me!" begged Flossie.

"Nope! Can't!" answered Bert.

"Pooh! I don't care! We have a secret too!
Haven't we, Flossie?"

"Yes, and it's a nice one."

"Well, when it's time," went on Bert, "Nan
and I will tell you our secret and you can tell
us yours."

"That will be fun!" exclaimed Flossie.

"Only," said Freddie, "if we tell you our
secret you mustn't tell Mother or Father."

"We won't," Nan promised. "And now we
must get washed, for supper will soon be
ready."

The snow cream dessert was a great success,
and Mr. Bobbsey passed his dish for a second
helping.

"Who made it?" he asked.

"Nan," answered Bert, who was always glad to give his sister credit for good work.

"Oh, but Flossie and Freddie helped," said Nan quickly, smiling at the little twins.

"Good work!" ejaculated their father. "If they keep on they'll be almost as good cooks as Dinah is."

The supper was a merry meal as, indeed, were nearly all in the Bobbsey home, for the family, with the two sets of twins, was a very happy one and some member of it was always laughing or joking.

After the meal Mr. and Mrs. Bobbsey went out to call on a neighbor, leaving the children at home. Nan had some sewing she wanted to do, so she went to her room.

"You promised to tell us a story," pleaded Flossie.

"Yes, I know I did," Nan admitted. "But Lulu, coming this afternoon, took up so much of my time that I didn't get my sewing done."

"Come on out to the kitchen," Freddie urged his twin sister. "Maybe Dinah will tell us a story while we help her dry the dishes."

"Oh, that'll be fun!" cried Flossie. They

often helped Dinah in the evening and then the jolly, black cook would tell some of her stories of the South where she had lived when a girl.

Flossie and Freddie were so taken up with helping dry the dishes and listening to the tale of a wonderful rabbit who could leap over a tall tree in one jump that they did not notice Bert going down into the cellar. It was not until Bert came up with a strange smile on his face that Flossie and Freddie looked at him.

Then, all of a sudden, Bert said:

"Well, I discovered it! I found it out!"

"Found what out?" Freddie wanted to know.

"Your secret!" chuckled Bert. "I found out the secret you two have been keeping down in the cellar!"

CHAPTER XIX

CAUGHT IN THE SNOW

SURPRISE, for the moment, kept Flossie and Freddie Bobbsey from saying a word to Bert. They could hardly believe what he said, yet they knew Bert always told the truth.

"Yes, I found out your secret, all right," went on the older Bobbsey boy. "Ha! Ha! You thought you had it hidden, but as soon as I went down cellar I discovered it."

At last Freddie found his voice to ask:

"Did you go down cellar on purpose to look for our secret?"

"No," Bert answered, "I didn't do that. I went down to get a piece of wood to fix my sled. It was when I was hunting around the wood pile that I saw the secret."

Flossie and Freddie looked sad and disappointed.

"But you won't tell our secret, will you?"

asked Flossie as she carefully put on the table a dish she had been drying. "Oh, Dinah! Don't let Bert tell!" she pleaded.

"Tell what, honey lamb?" asked Dinah as she came out of the pantry where she had gone to hang up her dish pan.

"Bert found out our secret—you know— the one down cellar," said Flossie. "You won't let him tell, will you, Dinah?"

"Ob course I won't, honey lamb! Look heah, Bert Bobbsey," she went on, waddling over toward the older boy, "yo' mustn't tell de secret ob yo' lil' brother an' sister. Don't yo' do it! Yo' heah me?"

"Of course I won't!" Bert quickly promised. "I don't tell secrets. But I guess," he went on, "you only want to keep it a secret from Daddy and Mother, don't you?"

"Yes, from them," said Freddie.

"Does Dinah know?" Bert inquired.

"Sho' I knows!" chuckled the black cook.

"Dinah helped us keep the secret," explained Flossie. "It's an awful nice secret, I think."

"Yes," agreed Bert, "it is a nice secret and

you needn't be the least bit afraid that I'll tell. But does Nan know about it?"

"No, I don't think she does," Flossie said. "I didn't tell her."

"Neither did I," said Freddie.

"Yo' all needn't look at me!" chuckled Dinah, her fat sides shaking as she laughed. "I didn't tell Nan."

"Then I think we might tell her," suggested Bert. "As long as I know it, there will be no harm in Nan's knowing. Mother and Daddy are the only ones you don't want to know."

"Yes," agreed Flossie and Freddie together.

"All right, then I'll tell Nan!" said Bert, and just then Nan came into the kitchen.

"Tell me what?" asked Nan, hearing her name spoken. "What's the matter? Has anything happened?"

"Oh, nothing much," answered Bert. "But just now, when I was down cellar. I found out the secret Freddie and Flossie have been keeping hid the last few weeks."

"Oh, so you discovered their secret, did you?" asked Nan, and she was much surprised. "Well——" She did not know what next to say. She knew how bad she would feel if some one found out a secret she had tried to keep. But Flossie and Freddie had now gotten over their first disappointment.

"Bert isn't going to tell anybody but you," stated Flossie.

"Mother and Daddy aren't to know," went on Freddie. "The secret is more for them than anybody else."

"Then it's all right," said Nan. "But what is it? Tell me the secret," she begged. "That is, if you really want me to know."

"Oh, yes, we'll tell you," agreed Freddie.

"And you can go down and look at it," added Flossie.

"Oh, how nice!" exclaimed Nan, with a look at Bert. "Hurry! I'm so excited!" she said, with a laugh.

Nan was, in a way, "putting on," to amuse the little twins, for she knew that any secret they had must be a very simple one. But it pleased them for her to think it was a big secret.

"Come on, I'll show you where it is," offered Bert, turning toward the open cellar door.

"No, let us show Nan!" cried Flossie.

"We can show her better than you can," added Freddie eagerly.

Nan gently held Bert back with one hand.

"Let them show me," she whispered as Flossie and Freddie darted quickly down the cellar stairs. "You know it's their secret, so let them show me."

"Oh, all right," agreed Bert with a laugh.

So the four Bobbsey twins went down cellar, while Dinah remained in the kitchen to finish putting away the dishes.

"Greates' chilluns in de whole world!" murmured the colored cook. "Dat's whut de Bobbsey twins am! Bes' chilluns in de world! An' Flossie an' Freddie sho' have a pretty secret. Ef dey can only keep it from dey Ma an' Pa till Christmas, it'll be all right."

"Whut'll be all right?" asked Sam Johnson, coming in just then and in time to hear Dinah talking aloud to herself. "Whut is it?"

"Nevah yo' mind, Sam Johnson!" she told him with a chuckle that set her to shaking again like a lump of cornstarch pudding. "Nevah yo' mind. Where yo' gwine?" she asked as she saw him start across the room.

"I's gwine down cellar," Sam answered.

"Not now yo' isn't!" decided Dinah, catching hold of him. "De Bobbsey twins is down cellar now wif de secret, an' yo' cain't go down! Yo' ain't got much sense, Sam Johnson, an' ef yo' saw dat secret yo' might talk in yo' sleep an' den Mr. and Mrs. Bobbsey would find it out. Yo' stay heah!"

"Dat's all nonsense!" grumbled Sam, but he knew better than to do something Dinah had told him not to do. So he did not go down the cellar to discover the secret Flossie and Freddie had so far kept so successfully.

"Oh, how wonderful!" murmured Nan, when she saw where the secret was hidden. "How lovely! How cute!"

"Won't Mother like that?" asked Freddie.

"Oh, I'm sure she will!" exclaimed Nan.

"And so will Daddy!" exclaimed Freddie.

"Yes, I'm sure he will," said Bert. "But you'd better not talk so loud," he cautioned.

"Why not?" Freddie wanted to know.

"Because Daddy and Mother might hear and come down to see what we are doing in the cellar," Bert explained. "Then they'd find out the secret ahead of time."

"Oh, that would be terrible!" whispered Flossie.

"Come on up!" begged Freddie. "You've seen enough of the secret," he said to Nan and Bert.

So it happened that two new persons were let in on the secret of the small twins. Flossie and Freddie were so excited about this that they did not think to ask Bert why he was talking to himself in the garage nor why he and Nan made so many trips to the music store down town. There was time enough to find out this other secret later.

Luckily Mr. and Mrs. Bobbsey did not return from calling on a neighbor until the twins, all four of them, had come up from the cellar. So the parents did not suspect anything about the secret Flossie and Freddie had arranged.

Christmas was drawing nearer. The school classes were to close for the holidays and on the last day there was to be no regular session. Instead, there was to be an entertainment for the whole school on the last Friday before the holidays.

Mr. and Mrs. Bobbsey had promised to

take the four children to this little show on Friday afternoon, there being no school in the morning. But when Friday morning dawned and Mrs. Bobbsey looked out to see snow falling heavily she shook her head and said:

"I don't know about going to the entertainment in this storm, children."

"Oh, the snow won't harm us," said Bert.

"It will be all the more fun," argued Nan.

"And if we go in the sedan we won't get cold," said Freddie.

"Oh, I love to ride in our car when it snows!" recited Flossie in a singsong voice. "It's such fun."

"Well, I must see what your father says," said Mrs. Bobbsey.

After Mr. Bobbsey had looked at the falling snow he decided that the storm was not bad enough to keep them home from the school play. So about two o'clock he brought the car around from the garage, the four children piled in the back, and Mr. and Mrs. Bobbsey sat in front.

"All aboard! Let's go!" called Freddie.

They drove along the shortest route toward the school, but the storm was worse than Mr. Bobbsey had thought, and when he got out into the open, away from the buildings, he found many drifts.

"I don't know whether I can break through that drift or not," he said to his wife as they turned down a road that led to the school. "I may get stuck." He pointed to a pile of snow.

"Haven't you chains on?" asked his wife.

"Oh, yes. But they don't always help. However, I'll try."

He speeded up the car and headed for the drift. For a moment it seemed as if they would plow through it. Then the auto slowed and soon stopped.

"We're stuck in the snow!" exclaimed Mr. Bobbsey. "And I think one of the tire chains broke. The storm is getting worse, too!"

He speeded up the motor and went into low gear, but the wheels only spun around and the car did not move.

The Bobbseys were caught in the snow.

CHAPTER XX

THE BEAR SONG

MR. BOBBSEY sat in the car beside his wife and looked out through the windshield and the glass doors at the storm raging about them.

"What are you going to do?" asked Mrs. Bobbsey.

"That's just what I was trying to decide," her husband answered. "We can't go on through this big drift, that's sure."

"Oh, shall we have to stay here?" asked Flossie.

"What if we do?" chimed in Freddie. "It will be fun to camp out here in the snow. It's nice and warm in our car."

"But I want to go to the school entertainment!" cried Flossie.

"Don't worry, we'll get there," said Nan.

"There is no danger of missing the entertainment," Mrs. Bobbsey assured Flossie. "At worst we can all get out and walk."

"Or hire a taxi," suggested Nan.

"Why don't you try to back out, Daddy?" asked Bert. "Maybe if you backed up a bit you could get a good start and break through the snow drift."

"I was going to try that," Mr. Bobbsey said. "I guess I will."

But when he put the gears in reverse and tried to move back, the rear wheels only spun around in the slippery snow as before.

"Both tire chains are broken," Mr. Bobbsey said as he shut off the engine. "The wheels can't get any grip on the smooth snow."

"Then what had we better do?" asked his wife. "I don't want the children to miss the Christmas entertainment."

"I'll get out and go to some garage and ask them to send a man with a jack and new tire chains," offered Bert.

"That's a good idea," his father said. "But I'll go, Bert. You stay here and take care of the folks," he added as he saw Bert about to object. "I can go more quickly than you as my legs are longer."

Flossie and Freddie laughed at this. But it was true. Mr. Bobbsey could make his way through the storm more quickly than Bert could.

"There is a garage not far from here," went on Mr. Bobbsey as he turned up his overcoat collar ready to step out into the storm. "They may have to bring the wrecking car to pull us out of the drift, but they can easily do that and once we have new chains on I can drive ahead all right."

"But won't we be late for the play?" asked Flossie.

"A little, maybe. But the play itself will undoubtedly be late," said her mother. "This storm is going to delay everybody."

"I made a mistake taking this back street," said Mr. Bobbsey. "On the main streets the traffic has kept the drifts down. But we'll soon be on our way," he added cheerfully as he opened the door, got out, and quickly closed it again to keep out the swirling snow.

As long as they could see him the Bobbsey twins watched their father battling his way through the cloud of white flakes that the wind tossed about and sent tingling against the glass of the auto doors and windows. It was warm and cosy in the closed car, however, and now that it was quite certain they would finally reach the school and witness their friends taking part in the entertainment, the children were all rather enjoying the situation.

"When will Daddy be back?" asked Flossie, after she had become tired of pressing her nose flat against the glass of the door on her side.

"Oh, pretty soon," her mother answered.

"Maybe they'll have to shovel us out of the drift," suggested Bert.

"If they do I'm going to help!" exclaimed Freddie.

"No, indeed," decided his mother with a laugh. "You're not going to get all wet in the snow and then sit through the entertainment. The men will have big rubber boots on and wading in the drifts won't bother them."

"Oh, I wish I had brought my rubber boots!" sighed Freddie.

"Yes, you'd look pretty, wouldn't you, wearing boots to the school play!" said Nan with a laugh.

"Well, I could take them off in school," Freddie said.

Five minutes passed, ten minutes, and Mr. Bobbsey was not yet back with the auto wrecker and the men to help put on new tire chains. Flossie and Freddie were getting restless and Nan, more than once, looked out to see if there were any signs of the rescue.

"Why doesn't Daddy come back?" asked Flossie more than once.

"Maybe he's stuck in a drift himself," suggested Freddie.

"Oh! Oh, dear!" gasped Flossie.

"Nonsense! Of course Daddy isn't stuck in a drift!" said Nan quickly. "Don't say such things, Freddie."

"Well, I was stuck in the snow once," Freddie announced. "It was almost over my head and Sam had to come and get me."

"I don't want Daddy to be stuck in a drift," declared Flossie.

Mrs. Bobbsey, too, was wishing her husband would come back and she was wondering what she could do to amuse the little twins when Nan suddenly called:

"Let's all sing!"

"What'll we sing?" asked Bert.

The twins knew several simple songs which they often sang together at home, with their mother to play the piano for them.

"Why not sing that funny bear song?" asked Nan's mother. "I always liked that song and you four do it very well, even without any piano accompaniment."

"Oh, yes! The bear song!" cried Flossie, smiling.

"That'll be fun!" exclaimed Freddie, who had been tracing the course of melting snow flakes as they ran down the glass of the doors. "And I'll growl like a bear," he added.

This was the part of the song he always liked to do.

"Get ready then," ordered Nan. "Sing your best, Flossie and Freddie! One, two, three! Go!"

The four voices were raised in the queer little song. The first verse went like this:

The old, black bear came out of his den,
  Boo! Bah!
  Boo! Bah!
And what do you think the bear did then?

Boo! Bah!
Boo! Bah!
He wiggled his head,
He waggled his tail,
He scratched his nose,
He twiddled his toes.
And what did the funny old bear do then?
Why, he went back and hid in his den.
Boo! Bah! Boo! Bah!
Boooo-oo-oo-oo!

Each time he came to the words "Boo! Bah!" that funny little boy Freddie Bobbsey growled instead of saying them. And his growl, as much like a bear's growl as he could make it, sounded very, very funny. At the end of the verse the four Bobbsey children burst into laughter in which Mrs. Bobbsey joined.

"How well you did it!" she exclaimed. "I never heard you sing it better. I always love to hear you sing that song."

Suddenly Nan seemed to have a new and strange idea. While her mother was talking to Flossie and Freddie, answering their questions as to which one of the two had sung best, Nan gave Bert a sly punch in the back.

"What's the matter?" he asked, quickly.

"Hush! Not so loud!" whispered Nan. "Don't let them hear!" She nodded toward Flossie and Freddie who, in their eagerness, were leaning over the back of the front seat, still questioning their mother to get her to say which of them had sung the bear song best.

"Oh, Bert, I have the grandest idea!" whispered Nan.

"What is it?"

She leaned forward and whispered something to him, her eyes alight with eagerness.

For a moment Bert was much surprised. Then, when he had gathered what his sister meant, his eyes, too, began to twinkle and he said:

"That's a fine idea! We'll do it! That's better than the secret we had first!"

"I'm glad you think so," said Nan.

Mrs. Bobbsey, who had at last managed to quiet Flossie and Freddie, turned to the older twins and said:

"I think you will have to sing the second verse of the bear song."

"Why, Mother?" asked Nan.

"Because Flossie and Freddie are teasing me to decide which of them is the better singer and I can't until I hear more. Come, sing the second verse."

The children did this, better than the first, raising their voices sweetly and in harmony. The music of the song carried above the noise of the storm, and a man who was beating his way through the swirl of flakes paused in surprise at hearing the melody coming from an auto stalled in the drift.

The second verse of the bear song ended.

"Didn't I sing best, Mother?" demanded Flossie.

"No, I did!" cried Freddie. "And I growled!"

But Mrs. Bobbsey did not have to decide the big question. For just then Bert, looking out of the back window, cried:

"Here comes Daddy and the wrecker! Now we're all right!"

CHAPTER XXI

CHUGGING through the snow, up came the wrecking auto with two garage men aboard as well as Mr. Bobbsey. The rescue machine came to a stop back of the stalled Bobbsey car and the children's father got out to make his way through the drift.

"Oh, I'm so glad Daddy is back! Now we'll get to the entertainment!" cried Flossie, clapping her hands.

"Pooh! I knew he'd come in time all the while!" Freddie said. As his father opened the door of his sedan to get into the driver's seat, the little boy eagerly asked:

"Do they want me to get out and help put on the chains?"

"No, little Fireman," answered his father with a laugh, giving Freddie the pet name by which he was often called. "The men will do all the work themselves. They have on big rubber boots and can wade in the snow. All I have to do is to steer our car when they pull us out."

"Are they going to put on new chains?" asked Mrs. Bobbsey.

"Oh, yes. Without them we couldn't go at all in this deep snow. I bought new chains in the garage where I hired the wrecker. The men will attend to everything. We'll soon be on our way and will get to the entertainment not much later than other folks, I think."

"That'll be good," observed Bert.

"Did the time seem very long while I was gone?" asked Mr. Bobbsey, as he waited for the wrecker men to attach a chain to his back axle to pull him out of the drift.

"I was afraid you'd not come back in time," sighed Flossie. "But I'm glad you did, Daddy."

"Yes, and I'm glad I came back to my little fat Fairy!" he said, gently pinching Flossie's chubby cheeks as he gave her the pet name she liked. "What did you do to pass the time?" Mr. Bobbsey asked.

"We sang," answered Bert.

"That funny bear song we like so much," added Mrs. Bobbsey. "I hope the children never grow too old to sing that song," she went on. "I like it so much."

"Yes, it's a jolly little song," agreed Mr. Bobbsey. "You must sing it for me some time."

Once more Nan gave Bert a sly punch in the back and the two older Bobbsey twins laughed and whispered together.

"What's the matter?" asked Freddie, observing this.

"What are you whispering about?" inquired Flossie.

But Nan and Bert did not have to answer, for just then the wrecker began to haul the stalled sedan out of the drift and the small twins were so eager to miss none of this that they quite forgot to question Nan and Bert about the new secret.

In a short time the sedan was in an open place where the rear wheels could be jacked up to take off the old, broken tire chains and put on new ones.

"All ready now, Mr. Bobbsey," called one of the garage men after a while. "You can go along now. I don't believe you'll be stuck in the snow again."

"I hope not," was the answer. "Thanks!"

The men were paid and chugged away in their big, powerful car. Mr. Bobbsey started his motor again and this time, with the new chains on, he had no trouble plowing through the drift. That place was the worst they met on the journey to the school, which they reached a little later, to find many others as late as themselves.

"We'll drive home by the main streets," decided Mr. Bobbsey as he parked his car. "Then we'll have easier going."

"The storm doesn't seem likely to stop soon," observed his wife.

"I hope it keeps up all night!" exclaimed Bert.

"Then there'll be a lovely lot of snow for Christmas!" said Nan.

"And we can go coasting!" chanted Flossie.

"And make a snow man," added Freddie. "Hurray! Hurray!"

Laughing and feeling very jolly after their little adventure, the Bobbsey twins hurried into the school, meeting many of their boy and girl friends who had also been delayed in coming to the Christmas entertainment because of the storm.

"Oh, I'm so nervous!" Grace Lavine whispered to Nan as they walked upstairs together to the big auditorium.

"Why?" asked Nan.

"I have to speak a piece," Grace answered, "and I'm afraid I'll forget some of it."

"Don't worry, you are a good speaker," said Nan. "You never forget in class when you have to recite."

"I know. But this is different—there's such a big crowd!"

There was a large attendance in spite of the storm. The affair was late starting, as Mrs. Bobbsey had guessed it would be.

But finally all the audience was seated and waiting for the curtain, which closed the front of the big platform, to go up. For once, at a school entertainment, the Bobbsey twins had no part in the program. They had all been asked by their teachers to recite, sing, or have something to do with a little play. But Nan and Bert had their secret to look after so they

declined, and Mrs. Bobbsey, though knowing nothing about the secret, decided that if
Nan and Bert were not to be in the entertainment, Flossie and Freddie might as well
be out for this once.

Then the entertainment began, and went
off very well. The older boys gave recitations,
and some of them, in Bert's class, put on an
athletic exhibition, swinging Indian clubs and
dumbbells. Bert wished now he had decided
to be in this. Then several girls in Nan's class
sang a song together, and some smaller children, in the class to which Flossie and Freddie
belonged, went through a march and drill.

It was when the second part of the entertainment was about to start that Miss Fletcher, the teacher of Nan and Bert, was seen to
be walking nervously up and down the aisles,
looking toward the doors and watching all
who came in.

"Oh, dear!" murmured Miss Fletcher as she
stood near Mr. and Mrs. Bobbsey who sat
with their children. "I'm afraid they can't
get here!"

"Who?" asked Mrs. Bobbsey.

"The Porter children were to sing a song in

this second half of the entertainment, and they aren't here yet," Miss Fletcher explained. "I'm afraid the storm has kept them away. I depended on that song to open the second half of our program."

"Can't you telephone and see if they are coming?" suggested Mr. Bobbsey.

"I have tried that," the teacher said. "There was no answer. The Porter family lives quite a distance out of town and I suppose they are snowed in. I don't know what to do without their song to start the second half."

Then Mrs. Bobbsey had an idea. She whispered to Miss Fletcher whose worried face lighted up as she smiled, and the teacher said:

"That will be splendid if they'll do it!"

"I'll ask them," offered Mrs. Bobbsey. "Children," she went on, gathering her four close to her, "don't you think you could help Miss Fletcher by singing the bear song? The Porter children haven't come and they were to open this second half with a singing number. Couldn't you do the bear song you sang so well in the auto?"

Flossie and Freddie were too surprised to speak. Bert shook his head and murmured:

"I'm not dressed to get up on the platform."

"Neither am I!" said Nan. "Oh, Mother! I wouldn't like to do it! We haven't practiced enough! Really I——"

"I think you do very well," said Mrs. Bobbsey. "Anyhow, this is an emergency and no one will care how you are dressed. Miss Fletcher will explain that you are filling in to help. You don't need any practice. Won't you do it?"

"To oblige me," added the teacher with a smile. "Please do!"

Bert and Nan could not resist this appeal. Flossie and Freddie were always ready to do what the older twins did and so it was soon arranged. The audience was getting a little impatient for the second part of the entertainment to start when Miss Fletcher stepped before the curtain and began to speak.

"Some of our entertainers have been delayed by the storm," she said, "so we have asked for volunteers. The Bobbsey twins have consented to fill in and will now sing for us the bear song."

There was a momentary hush and then the

applause broke out. The Bobbseys had many
friends in the school and all of them were
glad the twins were now to have a part in the
entertainment.

A bit bashful at first, Nan and Bert walked
up to the platform, followed by Flossie and
Freddie. But the children soon regained their
poise and, standing in line, they began to sing.

They sang the first verse as they had sung
it in the car, only much better. Then they began the second verse, a little different from
the first. It went like this:

The old black bear climbed up a tree,
Boo! Bah! Boo! Bah!
And what do you think he climbed to see?
Boo! Bah! Boo! Bah!
He opened his eyes,
He stuck out his tongue,
He sat on a branch,
He nibbled a bun.
But what did the funny old black bear see?
Why before he could look he was stung by a
        bee.
And then he fell Bump! down out of the tree.
Boo! Bah! Boo! Bah! Boo-oo-oo-oo!

You should have heard the laughter and hand-clapping when the song was finished! Freddie growled so loudly that he was red in the face, and Bert, Nan, and Flossie made such a funny "Boo!" at the last that the audience roared with laughter.

The hand-clapping kept up so long that Miss Fletcher, coming from the side entrance out on the platform, said to the happy twins:

"They want you to sing it again. They like it. Sing that last verse over."

This the twins did with greater success than at first.

"Oh, Bert," Nan whispered to him as they made their way back to their seats. "I think the secret will be better than ever now."

"Sure!" he said.

Flossie and Freddie were so pleased with their part in the bear song that they paid no heed to what Bert and Nan said.

It was still snowing when the entertainment ended and the Bobbsey twins started for home with their parents.

"I hope we don't get stuck again," said Mrs. Bobbsey as they got into the big sedan.

"No, we shan't," her husband said. "I'll keep to the main streets."

The car, with the new chains on, managed to do very well, and the family was almost home when Bert, looking from the window, called to his father:

"Stop! I just saw an old lady fall down in a snowdrift and she can't get up!"

"Where?" asked Mrs. Bobbsey.

"Right back there," and Bert pointed to the corner they had just passed.

"Yes, there is someone down in a drift!" exclaimed Mr. Bobbsey as he stopped the car and got out. He ran back, followed by Bert. Mr. Bobbsey lifted an old lady dressed in black.

"Why, it's Aunt Sallie Pry!" he exclaimed. "She is too weak to walk in this storm. Bert, you stay with her and I'll back up the car and we'll take her in. Poor Aunt Sallie!"

"No! No! I'm not looking for any alley," murmured the old lady who was very deaf. "I want to get home!"

"We'll take you home," said Bert, putting a supporting arm around her as his father hurried away to bring up the car.

CHAPTER XXII

NEW PLANS

MRS. BOBBSEY was all ready to help the old, deaf lady into the car as soon as Mr. Bobbsey had backed it to where Bert stood at the curb holding Mrs. Pry to keep her from again falling down in the snow.

"Oh, Aunt Sallie!" exclaimed Mrs. Bobbsey, "you shouldn't have come out in this terrible blizzard."

"What's that about a chicken gizzard?" asked Mrs. Pry, whose hearing was no better than the time when she had tried to help Nan keep house. "I can't say as I like the gizzard as much as I do the liver."

"Mother means," explained Nan loudly, as Bert and his father helped the old lady into the car, "that it's bad weather for you to be out."

"No, I'm not getting stout. Not a bit of it!" puffed Aunt Sallie. "I may look fat, but it's just because I have a lot of extra clothes on to keep me warm. Oh, it's nice in this car," she murmured as she sank down on the back seat, Flossie and Freddie making room for her between them. Bert and Nan had the two extra seats.

"Why did you come out in this snow?" asked Mrs. Bobbsey when they were ready to go on again.

"Yes, it is a terrible blow," Aunt Sallie agreed, and they did not try to tell her that she had heard wrongly. For, truly, the wind was blowing and it was also snowing. "I went out to mail a letter," Aunt Sallie explained, "and I guess I got turned around. I couldn't seem to find my way back home again."

"We'll take you there," offered Mr. Bobbsey, kindly.

"Thank you, I don't need a chair. This soft seat is quite good enough," said Aunt Sallie, laughing now.

Freddie and Flossie also wanted to laugh, for it was funny the way Aunt Sallie mixed up words. But a look from Mrs. Bobbsey made the small twins hold back their chuckles.

Aunt Sallie was a queer old lady. As you

have read, she once tried to help Nan keep house, but it was a funny failure. Later the Bobbsey twins were able to help Mrs. Pry get quite a sum of money. You may read about this in the "treasure hunting" book of this series.

"You should have stayed in," Mrs. Bobbsey said, as she helped the old lady dust the snow off her bonnet.

"Oh, yes, I have coal in my bin," announced Aunt Sallie. "Ever since you folks helped me get my property I've had plenty of coal in my bin."

Mrs. Bobbsey did not try to tell Aunt Sallie that she had said nothing about a coal bin. When Aunt Sallie got an idea in her head it was hard to get it out.

It was not much out of Mr. Bobbsey's way to drive past the house where Aunt Sallie was now living, and he soon stopped the car in front of her door.

"Bert and I will help you walk up to your stoop," Mr. Bobbsey said, assisting the old lady out. "There's a lot of snow on your stoop."

"No, I haven't any chickens in my coop,"

she answered, evidently thinking that was what had been said. "It's too cold for chickens in a coop now."

Bert tried not to laugh as he helped his father assist Mrs. Pry up the stoop. They opened her door with a key she had in her bag and the old lady was soon safely within shelter.

"Good-bye," Mr. Bobbsey called as he started to leave.

"No, I shan't cry," replied Mrs. Pry.

"And don't go out in the storm again," warned Bert.

"No. I haven't any pig in a pen," said the old lady. And she went to sit by her fire and get warm, quite sure in her own mind that Bert's last remarks had been about a pig in a pen instead of not going out in the storm again.

"Wasn't she funny, Mother?" murmured Flossie when Bert and his father had come back to the car.

"Yes, poor old lady! I'm glad we found her when we did."

"It was lucky Bert happened to see her fall," said Nan.

"She needs some one to look after her more carefully," Mrs. Bobbsey said.

"She needs an ear trumpet or something," remarked Bert. "She always gets words twisted."

"Still, she is quite a lively old lady," his father remarked. "But she should not have tried to mail a letter in this storm."

It was still snowing hard when the Bobbsey twins reached home. Sam put the car in the garage while Mr. Bobbsey went into the house with his wife and the children.

"Regular Christmas weather," he said, as he stood near a fire of blazing logs which Dinah had kindled on the hearth.

"And Christmas will soon be here! Goodie! Goodie!" cried Flossie, dancing about the room.

"I can hardly wait!" murmured Freddie. "Let's go down and look at our secret," he said to his twin sister.

"Wait until nobody sees us," she whispered back. "We don't want Mother or Daddy to find it out now. It's only a few days more."

So, watching their chance, Flossie and Freddie slipped down to the cellar while Dinah was getting the evening meal ready.

"Be keerful, honey lambs," she said to the little twins, "dat yo' all don't wear out dat secret by lookin' at it so much."

"Oh, it won't wear out!" said Flossie with a laugh.

When Nan and Bert had a chance to talk quietly by themselves, Nan said to her brother:

"What do you think about that bear song?"

"I like it," said he. "And Mother and Father like it, too, which is best of all."

"Do you think it would go better than what we have been practicing on?" Nan proceeded.

"A lot better, I think," was Bert's answer.

"Shall we have time to make the change?"

"Oh, I think so. We don't have to practice any on that song. We know it by heart."

"And Flossie and Freddie know it, too. Oh, say, Bert!" exclaimed Nan with shining eyes, "what do you say to taking them in with us?"

"On the secret, you mean?"

"Sure! The bear song secret!"

Bert thought this over for several seconds Then he said:

"I think it's a fine idea! Let's tell 'em and see what they say."

"Oh, they'll agree with us, I'm sure," said Nan.

After supper, when Flossie and Freddie again slipped down cellar to have a last good-night look at their secret, Bert and Nan followed. Mr. and Mrs. Bobbsey were entertaining visitors in the living room and there was no danger of their finding out anything now.

"Flossie and Freddie," began Nan, rather seriously, "Bert and I have something to tell you."

"You aren't going to tell Mother and Daddy our secret, are you?" asked Freddie.

"Of course we aren't!" said Bert.

"Bert and I are going to tell you our secret," went on Nan.

"And we're going to let you have a part in it," added Bert.

"Oh, goodie! Goodie!" cried Flossie.

"Say, that's swell!" exclaimed Freddie.

Then Nan and Bert whispered for some time to Freddie and Flossie, telling the small twins something that made them open their eyes wide with delight.

CHAPTER XXIII

WHERE ARE THE TWINS?

AFTER having covered all the country around Lakeport with a soft, fleecy blanket of white, the snowstorm stopped some time in the night. So the Saturday morning after the school entertainment the Bobbsey twins awakened to look out on a beautiful scene.

"This will make swell coasting!" cried Bert as he peered from a window before starting to dress.

"It surely will," agreed Nan. "But it will make it hard for us to go down town, Bert."

"Go down town—what for?" he asked. The older twins were talking back and forth from their rooms, the doors of which were open.

"Why, you know," said Nan in a lower voice. "What we talked about last night— the new secret with Flossie and Freddie in it."

"Oh, that! Yes, we'll have to go down town about that. But I guess the streets will be cleared by afternoon and that will be time enough."

"I think we ought to go down this morning," said Nan. "We haven't much time and it will take a couple of days to make the secret, I guess. Don't you think we ought to go this morning?"

"I'm going coasting with the fellows this morning," Bert said. "This afternoon will be plenty of time. Aren't you going to get out your sled?"

"No," Nan answered. "I'm going to help Mother and Dinah around the house. There's so much to do to get ready for Christmas."

"Well, all right," said Bert, hurrying to dress. "I'll take you all down town right after dinner."

"Are you going to take us?" cried Flossie, sticking her tousled head out of her bedroom.

"Sure!" answered Bert, making a dash for the stairs. He was in a hurry to eat breakfast and start for the coasting hill.

"What are you going down town for?" asked Freddie, as his head, as rumpled as Flossie's, came around the edge of his opened door

"Don't you remember?" asked Nan with a smile. "The big secret we talked about last night."

"Oh, yes!" Freddie exclaimed. "I almost forgot. Sure, I'll go down town with you."

"But you said you'd make me a snow man," objected Flossie.

"Oh, yes, that's so!" agreed Freddie.

"You'll have time enough for that," Nan told the smaller twins. "Bert and I shan't go down town until after dinner. Though I hope we'll not be too late," she added anxiously.

Bert had left the house when the other twins came down to breakfast. Mr. Bobbsey had also left for his lumber office. So Nan, Freddie and Flossie ate with their mother.

There were many mysterious looks, whispers, little spells of giggling and chuckles among the three children. Though Mrs. Bobbsey may have wondered what it was all about, she knew it was the Christmas season so she did not ask any questions which the children might not have wanted to answer.

"Where are you and Flossie going, Freddie?" Mrs. Bobbsey asked as she saw the small twins putting on their out-of-door things.

"Just to make a snow man in the back yard," Freddie answered.

"Oh, all right. But don't go away without telling me."

The small twins promised that they would not and then began the fun of making the snow man. The weather had turned warmer so the snow packed well and could easily be rolled into balls, which is the first start toward making a snow man.

Freddie rolled one ball and Flossie another. Flossie's ball was smaller than Freddie's. Then Freddie lifted Flossie's ball up on top of the one he had rolled and the hardest part of the work was done. The two snowballs formed the body of the white man.

"But we must put on his head," said Flossie.

"Yes. You make another ball, not as big as the first one, and that will be his head," Freddie suggested. "I'll carve out his legs and make some arms for him."

With a shovel Freddie began to divide the lower and larger snowball in the middle, shav-

ing away the soft snow. The man was soon
standing on two thick, white pillars, which
were his legs. Freddie made two long rolls of
snow, which he stuck on each side of the snow
man for arms. They extended straight out.

"It looks as though he was going to hug
somebody," said Flossie with a laugh as she
finished rolling the ball for the head. "Doesn't
he?"

"Yes, that's so," agreed her brother. He
stuck the snow man's head on his shoulders.

"We have to make eyes and a nose and a
mouth," said Flossie.

A lump of snow made a very good nose.
For eyes Flossie found two lumps of coal near
the cellar window beneath which was the secret she and Freddie had kept so well up to
now.

"This will make a dandy mouth!" Freddie
exclaimed, coming out of the house with a
piece of red cloth his mother had given him.

"Fine!" chuckled Flossie. "But he ought
to have a hat. I know where there's an old one
in the garage," she added. "It used to be
Sam's but he doesn't wear it any more."

With a hat on, the snow man looked, as

Freddie said, "very swell," and the little twins were admiring their work when a snowball which came from over the fence knocked off the snow man's hat.

"Oh!" cried Flossie.

"Who did that?" shouted Freddie.

Another snowball came whizzing through the air and knocked out one of the snow man's coal-black eyes.

"Hey! Stop that!" yelled Freddie. He ran to the fence and looked over in time to see Sammie Todd, one of the worst boys in the school, getting ready to throw another snowball. "Don't you throw at our snow man!" ordered Freddie.

But Sammie, with a laugh, hurled a third ball. It hit the top of Freddie's head, bounced off and knocked the other eye out of the snow man.

"Oh, you bad boy!" cried Flossie, who had looked through a hole in the fence to see who was doing this. "You bad boy!"

"You're mean!" shouted Freddie, though he was not at all hurt by the snow ball that had hit him. "Don't you dare throw any more."

"I will so!" declared Sammie.

But as he raised his arm to toss another ball, Sammie was suddenly caught from behind, thrown down, and rolled over and over in the soft snow.

"Oh! Oh! Stop!" he begged. "Stop!"

"I'll teach you to throw at my brother and sister!" shouted a voice, and there was Bert Bobbsey. He had come back from the coasting hill just in time to catch the mischievous Sammie. As Sammie tried to get up, Bert pushed him down in the snow again and rubbed some in his face so that the lad begged for mercy and promised never again to bother Flossie, Freddie or their snow man.

"You'd better not!" warned Bert as Sammie ran away.

"I wish I'd thrown a snow ball at him!" murmured Freddie.

"So do I!" echoed Flossie. "He was mean!"

"He won't bother you any more," said Bert. "Say, you have a fine man there!" he added as he saw the white image.

"Wait till I put his hat on again," said Freddie. The hat was restored, as were the eyes, and then the snow man looked as well as at first. Bert admired it and helped the little twins put a row of stone buttons down the front of the snow man to make it look as if he had on a coat.

"What'd you come home for?" asked Freddie of Bert. "Isn't the coasting on the hill any good?"

"Yes, it's fine. But it's almost noon and we have to go down town as soon as we eat. The secret, you know!" whispered Bert.

"Oh, yes," whispered Flossie, her eyes shining.

There were more whisperings, gigglings and queer looks among the children at the noonday meal, but Mrs. Bobbsey only smiled.

"We're all going down town this afternoon," Nan said to her mother when the table had been cleared.

"Be careful of autos and take care of Flossie and Freddie," warned Mrs. Bobbsey as the four started from the house.

"We will," promised Bert.

A little later the four twins were in the same music store where Flossie and Freddie had several times seen Nan and Bert.

"We wondered what you were coming here for," said Freddie, now that he knew the secret of the older twins and had a part in it with Flossie.

"It was Bert's and my idea," explained Nan. "But I'm glad we changed our plans so you two could have a part in it. I think it will be much nicer this way."

"So you aren't going to do what you first thought; is that it?" asked Mr. Necker, who kept the store. He had come out from a back room as the twins entered.

"We have thought of something much better," said Bert. "Listen to this," and as he nodded the others joined him in singing the bear song.

"Oh, that's a lot better!" decided Mr. Necker after he had listened to the second verse. "That will make a fine one! Come back into the studio and I'll give you a test."

Flossie and Freddie wondered much over what they saw in the studio, or workshop, of Mr. Necker. But they were soon so busy that they had little time for wonder.

Mr. Necker helped the Bobbsey twins prepare their wonderful secret. He made them do the bear song over several times before he was satisfied.

"Come back again Monday," he told the children, "and I think we can finish it."

"It won't cost much, will it?" asked Bert, anxiously.

"No more than I told you at first," said the music store man.

"I have ten cents in my bank," boasted Freddie.

"I guess we won't need your money," laughed Nan.

The twins did not tell their mother where they had been when they reached home. Mrs. Bobbsey did not ask them.

Monday came, and once more the four twins started for down town.

"My, such busy little people!" exclaimed Mrs. Bobbsey when she saw them go. "Don't stay too late," she warned.

"We won't!" promised Nan.

Mr. Necker was ready for the twins and they spent a busy hour in his music studio and shop. The time passed quickly and it was later than Bert and Nan realized. Outside it began to snow and get dark, but the Bobbsey twins did not know this. They were busy making a wonderful secret. At last Mr. Necker said:

"There you are. It is finished."

"Now we must hurry home!" exclaimed Nan.

Away they started through the storm and darkness, Bert carrying a small package.

Mr. Bobbsey reached home from his office.

"Why, aren't the children home yet?" asked his wife who came in just as he arrived, having been to call on a neighbor.

"I don't hear them," Mr. Bobbsey said, "and that's a pretty good sign they aren't in. Did they go out?"

"They all went down town early this afternoon," said Mrs. Bobbsey with a worried note in her voice. "Shopping, I suppose. But they ought to be home now. It's dark."

"And snowing," said her husband. "Dinah," he called, "do you know where the children are?"

"Why, no, I don't," she answered. "Oh, mah goodness! where am mah honey lambs? Out in de dark an' de snow!"

"I'd better go to look for them," said Mr. Bobbsey as he listened to the howl of the wind and the swish of the snow around the house. "They ought not to be out in this storm!"

"Dear me! Where can they have gone?" murmured his wife.

CHAPTER XXIV

SAFE FROM THE STORM

FLOSSIE and Freddie Bobbsey, with Bert and Nan walking ahead to shelter the smaller twins somewhat, were working their way through the storm. It was a sudden and hard blow of wind and whirl of snow that the Bobbsey children had to face when leaving the music store and studio of Mr. Necker. But under his arm Bert carefully carried the wonderful secret. It had been doubly wrapped to make it safe from the storm.

"Say, this is fierce!" exclaimed Bert as the wind whipped a lot of snow into his face.

"It's a worse storm than the one we were stalled in when going to the school entertainment," agreed Nan.

"I think it's fun!" said Freddie, trying to laugh, but the wind almost took his breath away when he opened his mouth, so he couldn't.

It was fun at first tramping on through the storm. The twins were so delighted at having finished the secret for their father and mother that they thought little of the blustering wind and the stinging snow. Besides the secret which Flossie and Freddie had helped the older twins get ready, there was the special little secret of their own which the two small twins had hidden in the cellar.

Two secrets for Christmas! Never had the twins had such delightful thoughts to occupy their minds. It was worth struggling through the storm for.

But as they tramped along in the darkness, for night had now fallen, first Flossie began to get tired and fretful, and then Freddie, brave little "fireman" that he was often called, began to wish he was safely home.

"Maybe we ought to have taken a taxi," suggested Nan as she helped Flossie out of a small drift.

"It's too late for that now," said Bert. "It would have been better, I guess, but there aren't any taxi cabs around here." He turned to look down the street. They had left the business part of Lakeport and were now on a residence street.

"It isn't much farther, is it?" asked Nan. "I declare, the snow is so thick I hardly know where I am."

"No, it isn't much farther," Bert said, peering up at a street sign when they came to a corner. "We're on Hedden place at the corner of Wright avenue."

"Oh, then it's nearly ten blocks more!" sighed Nan.

"But they're short blocks," Bert said. "Come on!"

So they pushed their way through the storm, the little twins getting more and more tired and cold. Still they did not complain very much.

Freddie held his little sister's hand and guided her as best he could. Bert and Nan, walking in front, the wind in their faces, served, somewhat, to keep the cold blasts off the younger twins.

At last Flossie gave a despairing cry and sank down in the snow.

"Oh, dear! Oh, dear! Oh, dear!" she sobbed

"Why, what's the matter?" asked Nan, turning in alarm.

"Oh, I've lost one of my rubbers, and there's a lot of snow down my neck and I'm cold and—and—I want to go home!" cried Flossie.

"We're almost there," Freddie tried to comfort her.

But Nan took a sudden resolve.

"Bert," she said, "we must take them in the nearest house and then telephone home. Daddy or Sam can come and get us in the car."

"Yes, I guess that's the best thing to do," Bert agreed. "We'll go in here," and he pointed to the house in front of which Flossie had sat down in a drift after losing her rubber.

There was such a whirl of snow that for the moment neither Bert nor Nan recognized the house up the steps of which they tramped, leading their brother and sister. But Freddie recognized it and he exclaimed:

"Aunt Sallie Pry lives here!"

"Why, so she does!" agreed Nan when she

saw the number. "Oh, we couldn't have come to a better place!"

She rang the bell, and the housekeeper, whom Aunt Sallie had hired to live with her after getting her "treasure," came to the door. She knew the children and welcomed them.

"Oh, you poor dears!" she exclaimed. "Come in out of the storm! I hope you didn't freeze!"

"What's that?" exclaimed Aunt Sallie, coming into the hall. "Some one with bees? Well, we don't want any! Bees sting!"

"No! No! It's the Bobbsey twins!" said Mrs. Bell, the housekeeper, now speaking loudly enough for Aunt Sallie's deaf ears. "I said I hoped they didn't freeze."

"Oh, freeze! Why didn't you say so at first," complained Aunt Sallie. "No, indeed, I hope they aren't frozen. But come in where it's warm. Why are you out in this storm?"

"We—we just went to the store," said Nan.

"You fell on the floor? That's too bad," said Aunt Sallie. "How did it happen?"

"No! No! *Store!*" and Nan spoke loudly.

"Oh, you been to the store, eh? Well, I'm

glad you stopped in out of the storm. It's a worse one than your pa took me out of."

"May we use your telephone?" asked Bert. "We want to tell my father we are here."

"No! No! There's nothing the matter with my ear," said Aunt Sallie. "Sometimes I can't hear as good as others, but there's nothing the matter with my ear."

"The telephone is in the next room," said Mrs. Bell, not taking the trouble to explain to the deaf old lady. "Yes, it will be better for your folks to come after you."

So a little later, just when Mr. Bobbsey, as much worried as his wife was, prepared to set off in search of the children, the telephone rang and Bert told his father that they were all safe from the storm in Aunt Sallie's house.

"Oh, I'm so glad!" sighed Mrs. Bobbsey. "Go after them at once in the sedan and let Sam drive."

The car was soon at the old lady's house, and the twins, after bidding her good-bye and wishing her a Merry Christmas, rode home with their father.

"What made you go down town in such a storm?" asked Mr. Bobbsey.

"It wasn't snowing when we went," answered Bert, taking care to hide the package he carried so his father wouldn't see it.

"Well, I'm glad you went into Aunt Sallie's. Your mother and I were getting worried about you."

"It was fun, though," said Freddie, when they were snug and warm at home. "I liked the storm."

"I didn't. It tickled my neck and I lost a rubber," said Flossie.

It stormed all night.

"But who cares?" cried Bert when he jumped out of bed the next morning. "To-morrow is Christmas!"

"To-morrow is Christmas!" echoed the small twins.

"Oh, won't it be wonderful!" exclaimed Nan.

"Then we can tell our secret!" laughed Flossie.

CHAPTER XXV

MERRY CHRISTMAS SECRETS

Such a long day it seemed—that one before Christmas. But it was most delightful. The storm slowly blew itself out, but the whole country was covered with a blanket of white.

"Regular Christmas weather!" everybody said.

The Bobbsey twins hurried here and there about the house, Bert helping with putting up the holly trimming, Nan busy helping Dinah and her mother in the kitchen. Flossie and Freddie went up and down the cellar steps so many times that Dinah said:

"'Tis a wonder dey don't wear out dem steps!"

In the afternoon all the children went coasting on the hill, for it was fine for sleds. Everybody was talking about Christmas and merry shouts and laughter were heard on all sides.

The sun began to go down and night came on.

"Christmas eve!" whispered Flossie, wonderingly.

"Oh, I can hardly wait until to-morrow!" sighed Freddie.

"Is it put away safe, Bert?" asked Nan.

"What?"

"The—the secret."

"Sure! It's hid in my room. We'll give it to 'em in the morning."

"Christmas morning!" murmured Nan, joyfully.

"And we'll give 'em our secret, too," said Flossie.

"I hope Mother will like it," said Freddie.

The Bobbsey twins went to bed at last. The Christmas tree had been trimmed.

"But I'm sure I'll never get to sleep," sighed Nan.

But she did, and so did Bert and Flossie and Freddie.

Christmas morning dawned, but long before the sun was out of its bed in the clouds there were movements in the rooms of the twins; the shuffling of bare feet, the whispering of smiling lips, the snapping on and off of lights.

Mr. and Mrs. Bobbsey heard these noises in their room.

"What's going on?" called Mr. Bobbsey.

"Merry Christmas! Merry Christmas! Merry Christmas! Merry Christmas!" Four joyous voices shouted this happy greeting.

"Oh, is it Christmas?" asked Mr. Bobbsey.

"Just as if you didn't know!" laughed Nan. "Ho! Ho!"

"May we go down and look at our presents?" asked Flossie.

"Oh, I guess so," their mother answered.

"And then we want you and Daddy to come down and look at what Santa Claus brought you!" called Nan. "Will you?"

"Yes," her father said. "Run down to the tree. We'll be down in a little while."

"Put on your slippers and robes!" ordered Mrs. Bobbsey. "It's cold!"

"We will!" came in a chorus.

Such an excited rush as there was down the stairs!

Bert switched on the tiny electric lights that festooned the Christmas tree. On it and around it were the presents for the children and for Mr. Bobbsey and his wife. But not all the presents were there yet.

Bert and Nan were so taken up with their wonderful Christmas secrets, as were Flossie and Freddie, that they scarcely looked at their own gifts, fine as they were.

"Now, Flossie and Freddie, bring up your secret," said Nan as she heard her father and mother on their way downstairs. "Quick!"

"I'll help him carry it!" cried Flossie, eagerly.

The two clattered down the cellar steps and came up, carefully carrying something between them. Mr. and Mrs. Bobbsey were standing before the gay tree, smiling at the happy children.

"Shut your eyes, Mother! Shut your eyes, Daddy!" called Freddie.

"Then you can see your secret!" laughed Flossie.

The parents did as they were told. Flossie and Freddie stood in front of them, holding out a basket with a gay red ribbon on it.

"Now look!" shouted the little twins. "Look! Look!"

"Mew! Mew! Mew!" came from the basket.

Mr. and Mrs. Bobbsey looked at a mother cat and four little maltese kittens nestling on some soft rags. The mother cat looked up and purred. The little kittens mewed and crawled all over their mother.

"Oh, aren't they *darlings!*" cried Mrs. Bobbsey, leaning over to stroke the soft fur. "How lovely!"

"Real cute!" said Mr. Bobbsey. "Where'd they come from?"

"That's our secret Christmas present to you," said Freddie, proudly.

"We've taken care of 'em down cellar ever since they came," said Flossie. "They didn't get cold 'cause we put Sam's old auto shawl over 'em at night."

"So that was why you two went up and down so many times, is it?" asked Mrs. Bobbsey with a laugh.

"That's it!" Freddie answered. "This mother cat and her kittens came to live in our cellar quite a while ago," he went on. "It wasn't our cat, but nobody else wanted it and

Dinah said she guessed we could keep it.
Then Flossie and I got this basket to put 'em
in and we said we'd keep the kittens a secret
and give 'em to you for Christmas."

"It's a lovely present," declared Mrs.
Bobbsey.

"We took your rose sofa pillow for the
mamma cat and her babies to sleep on," said
Flossie. "But when you made such a fuss
about it, Mother, Dinah said we'd better put
it back. So we did. She cleaned it for us 'cause
it got dirty when I dropped it on the cellar
floor."

"So that's where my best sofa pillow went,
was it?" asked Mrs. Bobbsey with a laugh.

"And that's where my orange tie went,
too," said Nan. "They had tied it in a bow
on the handle of the basket."

"I didn't think the tie was any good," murmured Freddie.

"The idea! My best one!" exclaimed Nan.
"I took it away and gave them an old red
bow—after Bert and I found out what their
secret was," she concluded.

"We wanted the basket to look nice for
Christmas," said Flossie.

"Well, I'm sure it looks lovely," Mrs. Bobbsey agreed. "Oh, what a wonderful Christmas this is going to be!"

"But there's something else!" Flossie cried, looking at Nan and Bert. "Isn't there?"

"Lots more," said Bert.

"What! More secrets?" asked his mother.

"Oh, just wait!" cried Freddie.

Bert had slipped into the room back of the Christmas tree. There was a clicking noise and then there came echoing forth the words of the bear song, with tinkling piano music for an accompaniment.

The old black bear came out of his den.
   Boo! Bah! Boo! Bah!
And what do you think the bear did then?
   Boo! Bah! Boo! Bah!
He wiggled his head,
He waggled his tail,
He scratched his nose,
He twiddled his toes.
And what did the funny old bear do then?
Why, he went back and hid in his den.
   Boo! Bah! Boo! Bah!
   Boooo-oo-oo-oo!

Though the four Bobbsey twins were in the Christmas tree room with their mother and father, their voices seemingly came from the back room. The sweet soprano of Flossie and Nan mingled with the clear tones of Bert's boyish voice, and, here and there, Freddie could be heard to growl, just as he had done when he sang in the snow-stalled car and at the school entertainment.

With the singing of the second verse about the funny bear the song came to an end. Mr. and Mrs. Bobbsey looked at each other with questions in their eyes.

"Say, that's great!" cried Mr. Bobbsey.

"How wonderful!" murmured his wife. "How did you ever do it, my dears? Is it the radio?"

"It's a phonograph record for you and Daddy for Christmas!" cried Bert, unable to keep still any longer.

"And I sang into a funny horn!" exclaimed Flossie.

"I helped make it, too!" added Freddie.

"That's our Christmas secret," said Nan, smiling, "Bert's and mine, just as the basket of kittens came from Flossie and Freddie."

"A phonograph record!" cried Mrs. Bobbsey. "How fine! And I can keep it always and hear your voices in the bear song Daddy and I love so, even after you are grown up! It's the most wonderful Christmas present we ever had, isn't it, Daddy?"

"I'll say it is!" he cried, catching Freddie and Flossie up in his arms.

"How did you do it?" asked Mrs. Bobbsey, as she kissed Nan and Bert, thanking them again and again for the gift.

"Oh, Bert and I thought it up," Nan explained. "First we were going to make a phonograph record of a dialogue he and I did in school. So we practiced that out in the garage. It was a quarreling sort of dialogue."

"And we heard you!" said Freddie. "Nan said 'it can't be done.'"

"And Bert said it must be done," added Flossie. "We didn't know what it was, but we thought it was queer."

"Yes, Nan and I had all we could do to keep the secret away from them," Bert explained. "But after we had sung the bear song in the car we thought that would sound better on a phonograph record than a quarreling dialogue. And then we decided to let Flossie and Freddie in on the secret because they could sing with us. So we did. Anyhow, we already knew their secret about the kittens."

"So that's why they were going down cellar so much!" chuckled Mrs. Bobbsey. "To feed the kittens and keep them warm with my rose sofa pillow! Oh, you little tykes!"

"But after Dinah made us take the pillow away we got an old shawl and things like that to put in the basket," Flossie said.

"Play that bear song record again," begged Mr. Bobbsey.

When they had all listened, after Bert had once more wound up the phonograph in the other room, Mrs. Bobbsey said:

"But I don't understand how you children could have a record made of your voices. Did you get only one?"

"That's all," Bert said. "It isn't like a regular record made in a factory. Mr. Necker has a machine that makes small records for the home right in his music shop studio. He put a soft metal disk on a machine that kept turning it around, and then we sang into a horn that had a sort of sound box and a needle on the disk end. The needle made dents in the disk and when you play it the song comes out."

"It's very wonderful," said Mrs. Bobbsey. "I didn't know you could make family records that way. I knew you and Nan were up to some trick," she said to Bert, "going out to the garage so often and then slipping away down town, but I never guessed that you were making a phonograph record."

"It took a lot of practice," Nan said, "especially when we had the first idea of the dialogue. But it was easier after we four sang the bear song together. We didn't have to practice but once or twice for that. And we finished the record and brought it home that day we were caught in the storm and went into Aunt Sallie's."

"Ha! Ha! They fooled us all right, Mother!" chuckled Mr. Bobbsey, looking at his wife. "The Bobbsey twins certainly know how to keep secrets! Oh, what a wonderful Christmas this is!"

"I wonder if we'll ever have another as good?" murmured Nan as she looked at some of her presents.

Whether they did or not remains to be seen. Soon they have fun another way, told in "The Bobbsey Twins at the Circus."

And, now that the two secrets had been told and the kittens had been set in a quiet corner with the mother cat and the phonograph record played again, it was time for the children to see what they had for Christmas.

"Oh, look!" cried Freddie. "Here's that hook and ladder truck I was looking at in the store. Golly gosh! This is great! Now I can be a real fireman!" He began to drag the apparatus about the room.

"And see what I got!" cried Flossie. "A doll that talks! The same one I touched in the store and she spoke to me! Oh, isn't it wonderful!"

"The best Christmas ever!" exclaimed Bert as he looked at a set of books he had long wished for.

"That's what I say!" chimed in Nan. "This bureau set is just what I wanted," and she flashed the handsome mirror in the lights of the Christmas tree.

There were also presents for Daddy and

Mother, and of course gifts for Sam and Dinah who were called in to receive them.

"Dinah was the only one who knew the secret about the kittens for a long while, weren't you, Dinah?" asked Freddie.

"Guess I was, honey lamb," she murmured. "But when yo' ma made sech a fuss about that rose piller, why I sho' done thought dat de secret was done fo', good an' all!"

"Listen to this, Dinah!" called Bert, starting the phonograph again. As the words of the bear song echoed through the room Dinah opened her eyes wide and exclaimed: "Good lan' ob massy! Dat sho' am wonderful!"

Then the Bobbsey twins sang the song themselves, the golden sun came peeping through the frosty windows and shone on the glittering snow outside, and Christmas Day had arrived.

THE END